ON THE TRAIL
OF PONTIAC

Or, The Pioneer Boys of The Ohio

I0542071

EDWARD STRATEMEYER

1st WORLD
LIBRARY
Literary Society

On the Trail of Pontiac

Edward Stratemeyer

© 1st World Library, 2007
PO Box 2211
Fairfield, IA 52556
www.1stworldlibrary.com
First Edition

LCCN: 2007901775

Softcover ISBN: 978-1-4218-4243-1
Hardcover ISBN: 978-1-4218-4145-8
eBook ISBN: 978-1-4218-4341-4

Purchase *"On the Trail of Pontiac"*
as a traditional bound book at:
www.1stWorldLibrary.com/purchase.asp?ISBN=978-1-4218-4243-1

1st World Library is a literary, educational organization
dedicated to:

- Creating a free internet library of downloadable ebooks

- Hosting writing competitions and offering book
publishing scholarships.

Interested in more 1st World Library books?
contact: literacy@1stworldlibrary.com
Check us out at: www.1stworldlibrary.com

1st World Library Literary Society

Giving Back to the World

"If you want to work on the core problem, it's early school literacy."

- James Barksdale, former CEO of Netscape

"No skill is more crucial to the future of a child, or to a democratic and prosperous society, than literacy."

- Los Angeles Times

Literacy... means far more than learning how to read and write... The aim is to transmit... knowledge and promote social participation."

- UNESCO

"Literacy is not a luxury, it is a right and a responsibility. If our world is to meet the challenges of the twenty-first century we must harness the energy and creativity of all our citizens."

- President Bill Clinton

"Parents should be encouraged to read to their children, and teachers should be equipped with all available techniques for teaching literacy, so the varying needs and capacities of individual kids can be taken into account."

- Hugh Mackay

PREFACE

"On the Trail of Pontiac" is a complete story in itself, but forms the fourth volume of a line known by the general title of "Colonial Series."

The first volume, entitled "With Washington in the West," related the adventures of Dave Morris, a young pioneer of Will's Creek, now Cumberland, Va. Dave became acquainted with George Washington at the time the latter was a surveyor, and served under the youthful officer during the fateful Braddock expedition against Fort Duquesne.

The Braddock defeat left the frontier at the mercy of the French and the Indians, and in the second volume of the series, called "Marching on Niagara," are given the particulars of General Forbes' campaign against Fort Duquesne and the advance of Generals Prideaux and Johnson against Fort Niagara, in which not only Dave Morris, but likewise his cousin Henry, do their duty well as young soldiers.

The signal victory at Niagara gave to the English control of all that vast territory lying between the great Lakes and what was called the Louisiana Territory. But war with France was not yet at an end, and in the third volume of the series, entitled "At the Fall of Montreal," I have related the particulars of the last campaign against the French, including General Wolfe's memorable scaling of the Heights of Quebec, the battle on the Plains of Abraham, and lastly the fall of Montreal itself, which brought this long-drawn war to a conclusion, and was the means of placing Canada where it remains to-day, in the hands of England.

With the conclusion of the War with France, the settlers in America imagined that they would be able to go back unmolested to their homesteads on the frontier. But such was not to be. The Indians who had assisted France during the war were enraged to see the English occupying what they considered their own personal hunting grounds, and, aroused by the cunning and eloquence of the great chief Pontiac, and other leaders, they concocted more than one plot to fall upon the settlements and the forts of the frontier and massacre all who opposed them. The beginning of this fearful uprising of the red men is given in the pages which follow.

As in my previous books, I have tried to be as accurate historically as possible. The best American, English, and French authorities have been consulted. I trust that all who read the present volume may find it both entertaining and instructive.

EDWARD STRATEMEYER.

July 1, 1904

CONTENTS

CHAPTER I

A GLIMPSE AT THE PAST

"Two wild turkeys and seven rabbits. Not such a bad haul after all, Henry."

"That is true, Dave. But somehow I wanted to get a deer if I could."

"Oh, I reckon almost any hunter would like to bring down a deer," went on Dave Morris. "But they are not so plentiful as they were before the war."

"That is true." Henry Morris placed the last rabbit he had brought down in his game-bag. "I can remember the time when the deer would come up to within a hundred yards of the house. But you have got to take a long tramp to find one now."

"And yet game ought to be plentiful," went on his younger cousin. "There wasn't much hunting in this vicinity during the war. Nearly everybody who could go to the front went."

"There were plenty who couldn't be hired to go, you know that as well as I do. Some were afraid they wouldn't get their pay and others were afraid the French or the Indians would knock 'em over." Henry Morris took a deep breath. "Beats me how they could stay home—with the enemy doing their best to wipe us out."

"I can't understand it either. But now the war is over, do you think we'll have any more trouble with the Indians?" continued Dave Morris, as he and his cousin started forward through the deep snow that lay in the woods which had been their hunting ground for the best part of the day.

"It's really hard to tell, Dave. Father thinks we'll have no more trouble, but Sam Barringford says we won't have real peace until the redskins have had one whipping they won't forget as long as they live."

"Well, Sam knows the Indians pretty thoroughly."

"No one knows them better. And why shouldn't he know 'em? He's been among them since he was a small boy, and he must be fifty now if he's a day."

"I can tell you one thing, Henry," continued Dave warmly. "I was mighty glad to see Sam recover from that wound he received at Quebec. At first I thought he would either die or be crazy for the rest of his life."

"It's his iron constitution that pulled him through. Many another soldier would have caved in clean and clear. But hurry up, if you want to get home before dark," and so speaking, Henry Morris set off through the woods at a faster pace than ever, with his cousin close at his heels. Each carried his game-bag on his back and a flint-lock musket over his shoulder.

The time was early in the year 1761, but a few months after the fall of Montreal had brought the war between France and England in America to a close. Canada was now in the possession of the British, and the settlers in our colonies along the great Atlantic seacoast, and on the frontier westward, were looking for a long spell of peace in which they might regain that which had been lost, or establish themselves in new localities which promised well.

As already mentioned, Dave and Henry Morris were cousins, Henry being the older by several years. They lived in the little settlement of Will's Creek, Virginia, close to where the town of Cumberland stands to-day. The Morris household consisted of Dave's father, Mr. James Morris, who was a widower, and Mr. Joseph Morris, his wife Lucy, and their children, Rodney, several years older than Henry, who came next, and Nell, a girl of about six, who was the household pet. In years gone by Rodney had been a good deal of a cripple, but a surgical operation had done wonders for him and now he was almost as strong as any of the others.

James Morris was a natural born trapper and fur trader, and when his wife died he left his son Dave in the care of his brother Joseph and wandered to the west, where he established a trading-post on the Kinotah, a small stream flowing into the Ohio River. This was at the time that George Washington, the future President of our country, was a young surveyor, and in the first volume of this series, entitled "With Washington in the West," I related how Dave fell in with Washington and became his assistant, and how, later on, Dave became a soldier to march under Washington during the disastrous Braddock campaign against Fort Duquesne.

General Braddock's failure to bring the French to submission cost James Morris dearly. His trading-post was attacked and he barely escaped with his life. Dave likewise became a prisoner of the enemy, and it was only through the efforts of a friendly Indian named White Buffalo, and an old frontier acquaintance named Sam Barringford, that the pair escaped to a place of safety.

War between France and England had then become a certainty. France was aided greatly by the Indians, and it was felt by the colonists that a strong blow must be struck and without delay. Expeditions against the French were organized, and in the second volume of the series, called "Marching on Niagara," are given the particulars of another campaign against Fort Duquesne (located where the city of Pittsburg, Penn., now stands) and then of the long and hard campaign against Fort Niagara. Dave and Henry were both in the contest, for they had joined the ranks of the Royal Americans, as the Colonial troops were called.

With the fall of Fort Niagara the English came once again into possession of all the territory lying between the Great Lakes and the lower Mississippi. But Canada was not yet taken, and there followed more campaigns, which have been described in the third volume of the series, called "At the Fall of Montreal." In these campaigns both Dave and Henry fought well, and with them was Sam Barringford, who had promised the parents that he would keep an eye on the youths. Henry had been taken prisoner and Barringford had been shot, but in the end all had been re-united, and as soon as the old frontiersman was well enough to do so, the three had left the army and gone back to the homestead at Will's Creek.

It had been a great family re-union and neighbors from miles around had come in to hear what the young soldiers and their sturdy old friend might have to tell. Because of the ending of the terrible war, there was general rejoicing everywhere.

"I never wish to see the like of it again," Mrs. Morris had said, not once, but many times. "Think of those who have been slain, and who are wounded!"

Edward Stratemeyer

"You are right, Lucy," her husband had returned. "There is nothing worse than war, unless it be a pestilence. I, too, want nothing but peace hereafter."

"And I agree most heartily," had come from James Morris. "One cannot till the soil nor hunt unless we are at peace with both the French and the Indians."

"Be thankful that Jean Bevoir has been removed from your path," had come from his brother.

"And from our path, too, Joseph," Mrs. Morris had put in quickly.

Jean Bevoir had been a rascally French trader who owned a trading-post but a few miles from that established by James Morris on the Kinotah. Bevoir had claimed the Morris post for his own, and had aided the Indians in an attack which had all but ruined the buildings. Later on the Frenchman had helped in the abduction of little Nell, but the girl had been rescued by Dave and her brother Henry. Then Jean Bevoir drifted to Montreal, and while trying to loot some houses there during the siege, was shot down in a skirmish between the looters on one side, and the French and the English soldiers on the other. The Morrises firmly believed that Jean Bevoir was dead, but such was not a fact. A wound thought to be fatal had taken a turn for the better, and the fellow was now lying in a French farmhouse on the St. Lawrence, where two or three of his old companions in crime were doing their best to nurse him back to health and strength. Jean Bevoir had not forgotten the Morrises, nor what they had done to drag him down, as he expressed it, and, although the war was at an end, he was determined to make Dave, Henry, and the others pay dearly for the ruin they had brought to his plans in the past.

"I shall show them that, though France is beaten, Jean

Bevoir still lives," he told himself boastingly. "The trading-post on the Kinotah with its beautiful lands, shall still be mine—the Morrises shall never possess it!" Sometimes he spoke to his companions of these things, but they merely smiled at him, thinking that what he had in mind to do would prove impossible of accomplishment.

CHAPTER II

THE CABIN IN THE CLEARING

It was already four o'clock and the short winter day was drawing to a close. On every side of the two young hunters arose the almost trackless woods, with here and there a small opening, where the wind had swept the rocks clear of snow. Not a sound broke the stillness.

"Were we ever in this neighborhood before?" questioned Dave, after a silence of several minutes.

"Yes, I was up here three or four years ago," answered his cousin, who, as my old readers know, was a natural-born hunter and woodsman. "Got a deer right over yonder." And he pointed with his hand. "The one I hit plumb in the left eye."

"Oh, yes, I remember that," came from Dave. "It was a prime shot. Wish I could do as well sometime."

"You needn't complain, Dave. You've done better than lots of men around here. Some of 'em can't shoot anything at all. They are farmers and nothing else."

"Well, we'll all have to turn farmers sooner or later—after the best of the game is killed off."

"Has your father said anything about going out to his trading-post on the Kinotah again?"

"Nothing more than what you heard him say on New Year's day—that he would go as soon as the weather got warm enough, and it was considered safe."

"I wish I could go out with you. I really believe I could make some money, bringing in pelts,—more money than I can make by staying here."

"Perhaps you could, Henry, and, oh, I wish you could go!" went on Dave impulsively. "Wouldn't we have the best times, though!"

"The trouble is father wants me on the farm. There is so much to do, you see. While the war was on everything went to pieces."

"But Rodney can help now. He told me only yesterday that he felt strong enough to do almost anything."

"Yes, I've thought of that. If he can take hold, perhaps I can get father to consent. Did you say Sam Barringford was going?"

"To be sure. And so is White Buffalo. I suppose father will take not less than a dozen hunters and trappers with him and six or eight Indians, too. He says he doesn't want to depend altogether on strangers when he gets out there, and he hardly knows what has become of the most of those who were with him before."

"More than half of the crowd are dead, shot down either in the trouble with the redskins or in the war."

"I've been wondering if there is anything left of the trading-

Edward Stratemeyer

post. Father has half a notion that the Indians burnt it to the ground, and burnt the forest around it, too. If they have done that, he won't want to build again on the burn-over, but at some new spot where the forest hasn't been touched and timber is easy to get."

"Do you suppose they burnt the post Jean Bevoir had?"

"I reckon not. The Indians were very friendly with that rascal."

The youths had now come to the edge of the woods. Here was a well-defined trail, running from Will's Creek to a hamlet knows as Shadd's Run, named after an old Englishman who had settled there six years previous. Shadd and his family had been massacred by the Indians at the time of Braddock's defeat, and all that was left of his commodious log cabin was a heap of half-burnt logs.

Turning into the trail, the young hunters continued on their way to the Morris homestead. This itself was a new building, for the first cabin had also gone up in flames during the terrible uprising. On either side of the road were patches of woods, with here and there a cleared field. Soon they came in sight of a log cabin.

"Hullo, Neighbor Thompson!" sang out Henry, and in a moment a man appeared at the door of the house, musket in hand.

"So you've got back," said the man, and lowered his weapon. "What luck?"

"Two wild turkeys and seven rabbits," answered Henry. He reached into his game-bag. "Here are the two rabbits I promised you for the powder." And he handed over the game.

"Thank you, Henry, they'll make a fine pot-pie. Didn't see any deer?"

"No."

"Thought not. Will you come in and warm up?"

"I'm not cold."

"Nor am I," put in Dave.

Paul Thompson had been followed to the doorway by his wife Sarah, and the pair asked the two young hunters how matters were faring at home.

"We feel lonely here," said Mrs. Thompson. "In Philadelphia we had so much company."

"You must come over to our house more," answered Henry. "Mother, I know, will be glad to see you."

The Thompsons had come to that neighborhood the summer before, taking up a claim of land left by a near relative who had died. Both were young, and the husband had thought to improve his condition by turning farmer rather than by remaining a clerk in one of the Philadelphia shops. But the loneliness of the life was something neither had counted on, and both were glad enough to talk to a neighbor at every available opportunity.

"I am coming over in a week or two, to stay three days, if your folks will keep me," said Mrs. Thompson. "Paul is going over to Dennett's Mills on business."

"You'll be welcome," said Henry; and after a little more talk the young hunters went on their way.

"I'm anxious to see what sort of a farmer Thompson will make," said Dave as he strode along. "I don't believe he knows a thing about tilling the soil. He's as green as we should be behind the counter of a shop."

"He'll have to learn, the same as anybody else."

At last the youths came in sight of home. It was now dark, and through the living-room window they saw the gleam of a tallow candle which rested on the table.

A shout from Dave brought his father to the doorway. "Back again, eh?" exclaimed James Morris. "And tired as two dogs after the chase, I'll warrant."

"We are tired," answered the son. "But I reckon we could walk a few miles more if we had to."

"I see you didn't get a deer this time," came from Rodney Morris, as he, too, appeared at the doorway.

"Mercy on us, you can't expect them to get a deer every trip!" ejaculated Mrs. Morris, who was bustling around the big open fire-place preparing supper. "It's a wonder they start up anything at all around here, with all the hunting that's going on."

"We got two wild turkeys and seven rabbits," said Henry. "We left two rabbits at the Thompsons'. And, by the way, Mrs. Thompson is coming over in a week or two to stay three days. Paul is going to Dennett's on business."

"I'll be glad to have her here," was the mother's reply. "Poor dear, I know just how lonely she feels. Of course you said it would be all right."

"Yes, I said she'd be welcome."

"I'm so glad!" came from little Nell, as she brushed back the curls that were flying around her face. "Mrs. Thompson is so nice! She can tell the cutest stories!"

"A story-teller always makes a friend of Nell!" laughed her father. "Even White Buffalo can charm her with what he has to say when it comes to stories."

"White Buffalo is a nice Indian," answered the little miss promptly. "The next time he comes here he said he would make me a big, big wooden doll, with joints that would move, and glass beads for eyes."

"You won't fail to keep him busy, if he lets you," came from Dave, as he kicked the snow from his feet and came into the cabin. He threw his game on a bench and hung up his bag, musket, outer coat, and his hat. "Something smells good in here," he declared.

"You've walked yourselves into an appetite," said Rodney. He picked up the wild turkeys. "Good big fellows, aren't they? You've earned your supper."

The game was placed in a cold pantry, to be cleaned and dressed on the morrow, and then the inmates of the cabin gathered around the table to enjoy what Mrs. Morris had to offer.

It was a scene common in those days. The living-room floor was bare and so was the long table, but both were scrubbed to a whiteness and cleanliness that could not be excelled. On either side of the table were rude, but substantial benches, and at the ends were chairs which had been in use for several generations. In a corner of the room stood Mrs. Morris's spinning-wheel and behind this was a shelf containing the family Bible, half a dozen books, and a pile of newspapers which had been carefully preserved from time to time, including copies of the "Pennsylvania Gazette," edited by Benjamin Franklin, and also of the latter's publications known as "Poor Richard's Almanack," full of quaint sayings and maxims. Over the shelf were some deer's antlers and on these rested two muskets, with the powder horns and bullet pouches hanging beneath. Behind the door stood another musket, loaded and ready for use, should an enemy or a wild beast put in an unexpected appearance.

With no tablecloth, one could scarcely look for napkins, but a towel hung handy, upon which one might wipe his fingers after handling a bone. The dishes were far from plentiful and mostly of a sort to stand rough usage. Coffee and milk were drunk from bowls with narrow bottoms and wide tops, and sometimes these bowls served also for corn mush and similar dishes. Forks had been introduced and also regular eating knives, but old hunters and trappers like James Morris and Sam Barringford preferred to use their hunting knives with which to cut their food, and Barringford considered a fork rather superfluous and "dandified."

When all were assembled, Joseph Morris said grace, and then Mrs. Morris brought in what she had to offer—some fried bacon, a pot of baked beans, apple sauce made from several strings of dried apples brought from the loft of the cabin, and fresh bread, just from the hot stones of the fireplace. All fell to without delay, and while eating Dave and Henry told the particulars of the hunt just ended. It was not an elaborate meal, but it was much better than many of their neighbors could afford, and the Morrises were well content.

"I think you were wise to go out to-day," said James Morris, after the young hunters had told their story. "There is another storm in the air and it won't be long in settling down."

"It is going to be a long, hard winter, father," answered Dave.

"What makes you say that?"

"Henry said so. He found a squirrel's nest just loaded with nuts."

"Certainly a pretty good sign, for the squirrels know just about how long they have got to keep themselves in food before spring comes."

"I hope it stays clear for a day longer," put in Joseph Morris. "I am looking for Sam Barringford. He went to Bedford for me, and if it should snow, traveling for him will be bad."

"Sam won't mind a little snowstorm," came from Henry. "He has been out in the heaviest kind of a storm more than once."

After the evening meal, the whole family gathered around the open fire-place and an extra log was piled on the blaze. As nobody seemed to want to read, the tallow candle was extinguished and saved for another occasion, for candles were by no means as plentiful as some of my youthful readers may imagine. They were all of home manufacture and the making of them was no easy task.

CHAPTER III

BARRINGFORD'S STRANGE DISCOVERY

The new cabin of the Morrises, built after the burning of the old, was somewhat similar in shape to that which had been reduced to ashes. There was the same small bedroom at the north end, which, as before, had been turned over to Dave and Henry. But this room boasted of two windows instead of one, each fitted with a heavy wooden shutter, to be closed in winter or during an attack by the Indians.

The old four-post bedstead, of walnut and hickory, with its cords of rawhide, was gone, and in its stead the Morrises had built a wide bunk against the inner wall of the apartment, with a mattress of straw and a pillow of the same material, for feathers were just then impossible to obtain. Under the window was a wide bench made of a half log, commonly called a puncheon bench, and the flooring was likewise of puncheons, that is, split logs with the flat side smoothed down. Into the walls were driven pegs of wood, upon which the youths could hang their garments.

The room was cold, almost icy, and it did not take Dave and Henry long to get into bed after they had made up their minds to retire. Having said their prayers, they huddled close together for warmth, covering themselves with blankets and a fur robe James Morris had brought from his trading-post.

The wind had been gradually rising and by midnight it was blowing half a gale, whistling shrilly around the cabin and through the heavy boughs of the neighboring trees. The doors and shutters rattled and awakened Mrs. Morris, but the boys and men slept well, for the sounds were familiar ones.

In the early morning came a change. The wind went down and there was a heavy fall of snow which kept up steadily for many hours. By the time Dave and Henry arose the snow was several inches deep on the doorstep, where it had previously been swept clean.

"Traveling for Sam Barringford will certainly be bad," remarked Rodney, who was already at work, blowing up the fire for his mother. "If this keeps on, it will be a couple of feet deep by nightfall."

As there was but little to do that morning, Dave and Henry took their time in dressing. After breakfast they set about cleaning the wild turkeys and the rabbits. The feathers of the turkeys were saved and also the rabbits' skins, for all would come in useful, sooner or later, around the cabin home.

"The wind is rising once more," remarked Joseph Morris in the middle of the afternoon, after a trip to the cattle shed, to see that the stock were safe. "It is blowing the snow in all directions."

The boys had been out, trying to clean a path to the spring, but found their labors unavailing. So they filled a cask which stood in the pantry with water, that they might not fall short of this necessary commodity should they become completely snowed in.

Nightfall was at hand, and the wind was whistling more fiercely than ever, when Henry chanced to go to the door, to see if the snow was covering the cattle shed.

As he looked out he heard a faint cry. He listened intently and soon the cry was repeated.

"Somebody is calling for help!" he exclaimed to the others.

"Where?" asked Joseph Morris quickly, and reached for his hat and greatcoat.

"I think the call came from yonder," answered the son, pointing in the direction.

"Was it Sam Barringford's voice?"

"I couldn't make out."

"Perhaps some traveler has lost his way," put in Rodney.

"We can go out and see," said Joseph Morris. He went to the doorway. "This way!" he shouted. "This way!"

"Help!" came back faintly. "Help!"

"We're coming!"

Joseph Morris was soon out of the house, and James Morris followed him. Without delay Mrs. Morris lit the lantern and hung it outside of the doorway, that they might see their way back, and also placed a candle in the window. The fire was stirred up, so that the one in trouble might be warmed up and given something hot to drink.

With the snow swirling in all directions around them, it was no easy matter for Joseph Morris and his brother to move forward to the spot from whence the cry for help had proceeded. In spots the snow lay three and four feet deep, and to pass through some of the drifts was out of the question.

"Sam, is it you?" called out James Morris presently.

"Yes!" was the feeble answer.

"Where are you?"

"Here, by the old split hickory. Jest about lost my wind, too."

"We'll soon be with you," answered James Morris.

There was a row of brushwood to the south of the split hickory tree, and in the shelter of this the Morrises moved forward as rapidly as possible. The keen wind cut like a knife, and they knew that it was this which had exhausted the old frontiersman they were trying to succor.

Almost blinded, and nearly out of wind themselves, they at last reached the split tree, to find Sam Barringford crouched behind a mass of the snow-laden branches. He had a large pack on his back and also a bundle in his arms.

Sam Barringford was a backwoodsman of a type that has long since vanished from our midst. He was between fifty and sixty years of age, tall, thin, and as straight as an arrow. He wore his hair and his beard long, and his heavy eyebrows sheltered a pair of small black eyes that were as penetrating as those of any wild beast. He was a skilled marksman, and at following a trail had an instinct almost equal to that of the red men with whom he had so often come in contact. He was dressed in a long hunting shirt and furs, and wore a coonskin cap, with the tail of the animal hanging over

Edward Stratemeyer

his shoulder.

"Winded, eh?" remarked Joseph Morris laconically.

"Why didn't you throw down your packs and leave 'em?"

"Couldn't leave this 'ere pack nohow," returned Barringford, nodding at the bundle in his arms.

"Why not? Nobody is going to steal it tonight, I reckon."

"Taint that, Joe; the bundle's alive."

"What!"

"Babies—two on 'em, too."

"I vow!" put in James Morris. "Babies! Give them to me and I'll carry 'em to the house. Joe, you give Sam a lift, if he needs it."

James Morris took the precious bundle, while his brother relieved the old frontiersman of the pack on his back and took the latter's arm. The return to the cabin was made without delay, James Morris getting there some minutes before Joseph managed to arrive with Barringford clinging to his arm.

"Sam has brought a couple of babies, Lucy!" said James Morris, as he rushed up to the fireside and proceeded to open the bundle in his arms.

"I do declare!" gasped Mrs. Morris. "Babies! Where did he get them?"

"I don't know, but—Oh!"

The bundle had burst open, and there to the astonished gaze of all gathered around were presented to view two little fat and chubby boy babies, each about a year of age.

"Oh, the dear little things!" cried Mrs. Morris, snatching up one of them and hugging it to her breast. "Are you alive?"

For answer the baby boy set up a faint cry and this was immediately answered by a similar cry from the other baby. Then arose a grand chorus which left no doubt of the facts that the babies were alive and that each possessed a good pair of lungs and full knowledge of how to use them.

"Warm them up, James, while I get them some pap," said Mrs. Morris.

"Oh, the nice little babies!" put in little Nell, crowding close to touch the soft and somewhat cold cheeks. "And such pretty eyes, too, and such soft hair! Mamma, I think they are just too beautiful for anything!"

While Mrs. Morris was preparing some pap and some warm milk Joseph Morris arrived with Sam Barringford, and proceeded to make the old frontiersman comfortable. The water was already boiling in the big iron pot, and Barringford was given a glass of hot liquor which soon made him feel like himself once more. Later still he was served with a hearty meal, which he ate as if famished.

"Great babies, ain't they?" he said. "Beats all creation how I found 'em, too."

"So you found them?" put in Rodney. "Where?"

"On the road about three miles from this place—close to where the Chelingworth cabin used to stand."

"Did you find them in the snow?" queried Dave, with deep interest.

"I did an' I didn't. Ye see, they was wrapped in the bundle an' the bundle was tied up to a tree limb."

"And left there all alone?" cried Mrs. Morris, who was busy feeding the little ones.

"It was a case of necessity, ma'am. The man who had had the children had done his best by 'em, an' he couldn't do no more," returned Sam Barringford gravely.

"Tell us the particulars, Sam," said James Morris.

"I will. I was coming along the trail, fightin' my way as best I could in the teeth of the wind, an' feelin' bitter cold a-doin' of it, when I came to a spot where there had been a fight between a man, a horse, and some wild beasts—wolves, most likely. I couldn't git the straight of it at fust, but at last I figured out that the horse had gone into a hole, broke his leg, and pitched the man out on his head on the rocks. The man had had the babies in a bundle, and to keep 'em from gettin' too cold had put 'em in the tree instead of on the ground, or else he did it to save the babies from the wild beasts.

"The wild beasts had done their bloody work well, and man an' horse had been torn limb from limb. The man's skull was crushed, and it and part of the horse lay in a nasty hole, an' that's what makes me think both had the accident. The man had emptied his two pistols and used his knife, but it wasn't no use. The fight was ag'in him from the start."

"Horrible!" murmured Mrs. Morris, while little Nell and some of the others shuddered.

"I didn't notice the bundle in the tree at fust, but while I was takin' in the awful sights afore me I heard a strange sound. 'Sam Barringford, thet's a wildcat,' sez I to myself and swung my gun around putty quick. But it wasn't no wildcat at all, but them babies beginning to set up a howl. Maybe I wasn't taken back. It war the greatest amazement ever overtook me, barrin' none!" added the old frontiersman emphatically.

"Was there anybody else around?" asked James Morris.

"Not a soul. I looked everywhere, an' tried to git a shot at some of the wild beasts, but they had gone clean an' clear. Then I made up my mind the best to do war to get them babies to some shelter, or they'd freeze to deth. I didn't know ef other folks around here war to hum, so I made for this place. When I got to the split hickory I war so tuckered out I set up the yell you heard."

"Did the man have anything with him besides the babies?" asked Rodney.

"No bundle. But he had his pistols, the knife, a gold watch, some gold and silver, and some other things which I didn't pick up because of the snow an' the wind. Here are the things I did bring along," and Sam Barringford brought them forth from a bag he had carried and laid them in a pile on the table.

CHAPTER IV

SEARCHING FOR CLEWS

The others gathered around and surveyed the articles Barringford had brought along with keen interest. The money amounted to two pounds and six shillings, some in Spanish coin, but mostly in English. The pistols were English weapons, but the knife was such as could be bought at any frontier town in the colonies. The watch was a large, open-faced affair, and on the dial was marked, Richard Gardell, Maker, London, 1742.

"Hard to tell if he was an Englishman or a colonist," mused James Morris. "What of his clothing, Sam?"

"Almost torn to ribbons by the wild beasts."

"We'll have to go back to the spot as soon as the storm clears away," said Joseph Morris.

"You didn't find anything with the man's name on it?" came from Dave.

"Nary a thing, lad. But my search wasn't any too good, remember," answered Barringford.

"As soon as I saw the babies I started for here with 'em."

"Each has a locket around its neck," came from Mrs. Morris suddenly. "Perhaps they will give some clew."

"I trust they do," answered her husband. "That man may have been their father or otherwise only a servant sent to take them to some place. But, be that as it may, we must discover where the little ones belong."

"Oh, let us keep them!" burst in little Nell "I want some little brothers to play with!"

"Hush, dear!" came from the mother. "Mayhap the mother of these little ones is this moment mourning for them and wondering where they can be."

The lockets were small, oval affairs, rather hard to open until a thin knife blade was inserted between the two parts of each. One contained a miniature of an old lady in court dress and the other a portrait of an elderly gentleman, with powdered wig and gold-rimmed spectacles. The face of each was full of kindness and nobleness.

"Two fine old folks, I'll warrant," came from Joseph Morris.

"More than likely the grandparents of the little ones," returned his brother.

"The lockets seem new," said Rodney. "Perhaps they were christening presents, or given to the babies on their first birthday."

"The babies look very much alike and seem of an age," said Mrs. Morris, who had by this time fed them all they cared to eat. "I doubt not but that they are twins."

"Just what I was thinking," said Henry. "You had better remember which locket belongs to each, or you may get 'em mixed up."

"Mercy on us! I never thought of that!" exclaimed his mother. "Let me see,—yes, the first locket came from this one," and she hastened to replace it.

"There is a slight difference in their looks," said Dave, after a close survey of the two tiny faces. "One has a rounder chin than the other and a flatter nose."

"Dave is right," answered his aunt. "But the difference is not very great."

"Will you keep the babies for the present?" questioned Sam Barringford. "I don't know what to do with 'em, I'm sartin."

"To be sure we will," said Mrs. Morris. "Poor dears! if it was their father who was killed, it may go hard with them."

The matter was talked over during the meal and for two hours afterward, but none could reach any conclusion regarding the identity of the little strangers. All agreed that the best thing to do would be to look for more clews as soon as the weather permitted.

There was a large Indian basket in the cabin, in which Dave and Henry usually brought in kindling for the fire. This was emptied and cleaned and in it was made a comfortable bed for the babies to sleep on. Having satisfied their hunger and become thoroughly warm both slept soundly, nor did they awaken until early morning.

By sunrise the storm was practically over, although a few hard particles of snow still whirled down in the high wind. Joseph Morris said they had better wait an hour or two longer for the wind to go down, and this was done.

"Can I go along?" asked Dave eagerly. "I'm sure I won't mind the walk at all."

"I'd like to go, too," added Henry; and when the party started it consisted of the two youths, their fathers, and Sam Barringford.

The men took turns at leading the way and breaking open the trail, no mean task when in some spots the snow lay to a depth of four and five feet. They kept as much as possible in the shelter of the trees and bushes, where the drifts were not so high. The sun, shining clearly, made the scene on all sides a dazzling one. Not a sound broke the stillness, birds and beasts being equally silent.

It took over an hour to reach the ruins of the Chelingworth cabin—one of the first erected in that territory and burnt four times before it was finally abandoned. As they passed the ruins Sam Barringford came to a halt.

"Listen!" he said briefly.

All did so, and at a distance heard a sudden yelping, which gradually increased.

"Wolves!" cried Henry.

"You are right," answered the old frontiersman. "Reckon they have come back to finish their work."

"Let us drive them off," put in Dave, with a shudder. "If there is anything left of the man, we ought to give him a decent burial."

"Yes, lad, I agree; but there ain't much left but bones."

All pushed forward and soon reached the spot where Sam

Barringford had made his strange discovery. Five wolves were close by, sniffing eagerly through the snow, and more were in the rear.

"I've my shot-gun," said Dave. "Shall I give 'em a dose?"

"Yes," answered Barringford, and taking aim at two of the foremost wolves, the youth pulled the trigger of his weapon. The report was followed by a mad yelp of pain, and both wolves went down, one dead and the other badly wounded. The other wolves then ran off with all possible speed.

"A fair shot, Dave!" cried the old frontiersman, and striding forward he dispatched the wounded wolf with his hunting knife. "Doin' almost as well as Henry now, ain't ye?"

"Not quite as well as that," was Dave's modest answer.

The new fall of snow had covered all traces of the tragedy recently enacted at the spot, but the Morrises had brought along a pair of shovels and a broom, and soon the party was at work, clearing away the snow as Sam Barringford directed.

The remains of man and horse were at last uncovered, and then began an earnest search for some clew which might lead to the identity of the unfortunate person.

"Here is a gold ring," said Henry presently, and held it up.

Joseph Morris took the ring and examined it with care. There was an inscription inside, but it was so worn he could not decipher it.

They also brought to light several pieces of clothing, torn to tatters as Barringford had said. The horse's saddle was likewise there and the reins and curb, but absolutely nothing which gave either name or address.

"This looks as if we were stumped," said Henry, pausing in his labor of digging away the snow.

"Right ye are," came from Barringford. "Too bad! I'd like to know who them twins belong to."

"Reckon they'll belong to you, Sam," said James Morris, with a faint smile.

"Me! Well, I vum! An old man like me, all alone in the world, with twins! What'll I do with 'em? Answered me thet, will ye?" And he scratched his head in perplexity.

"We can keep them for the present," answered Joseph Morris. "Indeed, I don't think my wife will care to give them up in a hurry. She said this morning the youngsters had taken a tight hold of her heart."

"Ef I had a hum of my own—" began Barringford. "But no, 'tain't right—I ought to find out whar they belong."

"Perhaps you can find out all about them at Bedford, or Fort Loudan, or Annapolis, or Philadelphia," put in James Morris. "Certain it is they belong somewhere."

They had now come to the end of their search and, as there seemed nothing more to do, prepared to return home. The ground was too hard to permit of the burial of the remains of the stranger, and they were placed between some rocks, with other rocks over them, to keep off the wild beasts. Then Joseph Morris marked the nearest tree with a large cross and a question mark—a common sign of those days, showing that somebody unknown had met death in that vicinity.

When the Morris cabin was again reached they found the babies wide awake and cooing contentedly. Mrs. Morris had dressed them up as best she could, and she was holding one while Rodney held the other. Little Nell was dancing around the floor in wild delight.

"Oh, I just love those babies so much!" cried the little miss. "I want mamma to keep them, if nobody comes to take them away."

"Don't want to send them to the poorhouse, then?" questioned her father quizzically.

"To the poorhouse?" she repeated scornfully. "No, indeed!"

"What a fate for such darlings!" murmured Mrs. Morris. "No, Joseph, hard as times may be, I cannot consent to send these little ones away to live on charity, even if the authorities were willing to take them—which I doubt."

"Never fear, Lucy, I do not intend to be hard on the twins. And you must remember, Sam here has a claim on them."

"Oh, Uncle Sam," began little Nell—she often called him uncle—"won't you please let me keep the babies?"

The question was so gravely put the old frontiersman had to laugh outright. "A great question truly," he made answer. "And I don't know if they are mine yet."

"But if nobody calls for them—"

Barringford scratched his head.

"In thet case, I reckon as how I'll have to adopt 'em. Don't see nuthin' else to do."

"One thing is certain, they shall stay here for the present," said Mrs. Morris, and that important question settled, she turned over the baby she held to Dave, while she bustled about to prepare a late dinner.

CHAPTER V

A LIVELY ELK HUNT

The storm just passed proved to be the last one for some time to come, and in a week the trails leading from Will's Creek to the eastward became more or less broken. The trail to Fort Bedford was likewise opened, and Sam Barringford made a journey hither and was gone eight days.

The others awaited his return with great interest, but one look at his face when he arrived convinced all that he had failed in his mission.

"Can't find out anything about them twins," he said, getting down to what was in their minds without delay. "The man was seen around Fort Bedford for two days, but he didn't tell his business, and nobody that I talked to had seen the babies nor had they seen him a-talkin' to any wimmen folks."

"Where did he stop overnight?"

"Thet's something I couldn't find out, nuther."

"He must have been an odd sort," observed James Morris.

"Perhaps the twins didn't belong to him at all," suggested

Henry. "If they did, why was he ashamed to show 'em?"

Sam Barringford shrugged his shoulders and drew a long breath. "Don't ask me, Henry; it's a clar mystery, thet's wot it is."

Settling himself before the roaring fire, Barringford told his story in detail. He repeated all that the inhabitants at Bedford had told him, but this threw no light on the mystery. Nobody had seen the stranger come into the place and nobody had seen him depart.

"Wonder where he did come from," mused Dave. "He certainly must have come from somewhere."

After that the winter days passed slowly. Sam Barringford remained at the Morris home, occasionally going out alone or with some of the others in quest of game. He was always glad to have Dave and Henry with him, and they were likewise delighted to go, for, as my old readers will remember, Sam Barringford was a famous hunter and rarely came back empty-handed.

One day Henry, who had been out after wild turkeys, came back in a state of mild excitement. He had seen hoofprints which were strange to him, and he wanted Barringford's opinion on them.

"They looked something like a deer's," he said, "but were larger."

"Must have been an elk," answered the old frontiersman. "But I allow as how thar ain't many of them critters around this deestrict."

Henry had come back in the evening, so that the tracks he had discovered were not inspected by Sam Barringford until

Edward Stratemeyer

the following morning. The pair went out accompanied by Dave, and all were armed, and supplied with provisions enough to last two days, if necessary.

The way led up a small hill back of the house and then through a patch of scrub timber—the best having been cut away when the new cabin was built. Beyond the scrub timber was a small cliff of rocks and further still a dense forest, leading to the stream upon which the Morris boys had had such thrilling adventures in the past.

"Here are the tracks," said Henry, when the edge of the forest was gained. "And see, here is another trail made last night, I'll be bound!"

Barringford took his time at examining the hoof-prints in the snow, and at a spot where the sun came down warmly and made the ground slightly soft.

"Reckon I was right," he said. "Ef it ain't an elk, it ain't nuthin I ever seed afore."

"If it is an elk, let us try to bring him down by all means!" cried Henry. "I'd like a pair of elk horns very much."

"The trouble is, he may be miles an' miles away from here by this time," answered Barringford.

"Never mind, let us try it anyway," put in Dave.

All were on snow-shoes—Dave and Henry possessing pairs made for them by White Buffalo years before, and Barringford a pair he had traded in at one of the posts, giving some fox skins in exchange.

"I'm willing, lads," said the old frontiersman. "Even if we don't git the elk, we may stir up something else wuth knocking over."

He led the way directly into the forest, following the tracks of the game with ease. Dave came behind him, while Henry brought up the rear.

All was almost absolutely silent. Occasionally a winter bird circled through the air, or a frightened squirrel ran from a tree branch to his hollow, and twice they caught a fair view of a bunch of rabbits, nibbling at some tender shoots of brushwood. The young hunters could have shot the rabbits with ease, but now they were after larger game, and they knew better than to fire shots which would most likely drive the elk for miles, were the beast within hearing distance.

"How far do you calculate the elk is from here?" asked Dave, after a good mile had been covered.

"That's no easy question to answer, Dave," returned Sam Barringford. "He may have gone two miles and he may have gone ten. We'll have to trust to luck to catch up to him. I don't calkerlate he went far in this deep snow."

Another mile was covered, and they came to a spot where the snow was kicked up in several directions. A rough-barked tree was near by, and on this it was plain to see that the elk had rubbed himself vigorously.

"Thet proves he ain't gone far," said Barringford, almost in a whisper. "He stopped to scratch himself an' then dropped into a walk. Go slow now and keep quiet, an' we may come up to him before you know it."

The old frontiersman's advice was followed, and they turned along the newly-made trail, which now led up to the top of another hill. Here was a good-sized clearing, and Barringford motioned for the others to keep back until he could reconnoiter. They stepped behind some brushwood and each looked to the priming of his musket and to the flint.

Presently Barringford held up his hand and motioned for them to advance, but with caution.

"Reckon I've spotted him, but I ain't sartin," he whispered. "See thet hollow yonder? I think he's back of them bushes an' rocks. We had better spread out a bit."

The others understood, and while Dave went to the right, Henry moved to the left, leaving Barringford to advance as before. The hollow mentioned was nearly quarter of a mile away, yet so sharp were the old frontiersman's eyes that he had noted a peculiar moving of the upper branches of the brushwood before him, as if some large animal was tramping around, browsing on such tender shoots as the snow had not covered.

"If the elk don't go off like a streak, Henry shall have the first shot," Barringford had said, and it was arranged that, all things being favorable, Dave should shoot next, if a second bullet was required. Barringford would hold himself in readiness for the unexpected.

There was a cleared spot to cover, and at a signal from the old frontiersman they advanced across this, being all of a hundred yards from each other, and in something of a semicircle.

They made no noise, and the elk, for such it really was, did not notice them until they were within easy gunshot of where he was feeding. Then up went his head, to scent the air, and with a snort of sudden fear he started away, straight ahead of them.

Bang! it was Henry's weapon that spoke up, the instant he had the game out of range of the bushes. The bullet lodged in the elk's flank and he immediately began to limp. But he did not drop, and now it was Dave's turn to fire. Bang! went the second weapon, and the bullet lodged but a few inches below that sent in by Henry. On went the wounded creature, limping painfully, but still making good time, especially where the snow on the rocks was partly swept away.

"Come on after him!" yelled Henry, reloading with all speed. "I don't think he can get away!"

He had scarcely spoken when Barringford took aim and let drive. Strange as it may seem, the third bullet struck immediately between the other two. The frontiersman had aimed at the other flank, but the elk had jumped to one side, to avoid a hole, just as the hammer of the musket struck the flint.

Henry was running on as fast as his snow-shoes would permit, and having reloaded, Dave and Barringford followed. They were going downhill once more, but now the elk made a turn and darted into a belt of timber lining the river. Reaching the stream, he paused for a moment, looked despairingly at his wounded and bleeding flank, and then started across the ice.

When Henry reached the bank of the stream the elk was pulling himself up the steep bank on the other side. He now offered a fair shot once more and the youth was not slow to take advantage of it. Up came the gun, his gaze moved along the sights, and down came the trigger. But, alas! the flint was an old one and it failed to light the priming. Up came the hammer with an exclamation of impatience, but it was too late—the elk was once more out of sight.

"Why didn't you give him another shot?" demanded Dave, as he rushed up.

"The confounded flint wouldn't strike fire," growled Henry. "That's one of a lot I bought in New York when we were coming home, and they are no good."

"I'll see if I can't give him another," answered his cousin, and tumbled rather than climbed down to the river bank. Barringford came after him, and both crossed the stream and mounted the bank opposite. Here the snow was deep and both went into it headfirst, getting a liberal dose down their sleeves and collars.

"Oh, Columbus! but there's no fun in this!" cried Dave, as he brushed himself off. "Ugh! but that snow down my backbone isn't a bit pleasant!"

"Don't waste time hyer!" cried Barringford almost roughly. It made him angry to think that his first shot had not laid the elk low. "If you want to stay behind, why—"

"Not at all!" interrupted Dave. "I'm with you!" And away he went beside the old frontiersman. Henry had now adjusted a new flint to his musket-lock, and was following across the river as speedily as possible.

The forest was thick before them and they could hear the elk crashing along in a blind fashion, which indicated that he was speedily becoming exhausted. Once they heard him stop, but before they could reach the spot he was off again, at a still slower pace.

"We've got him now," said Barringford grimly. "Might as well slack up and wait for Henry."

He knew that Henry would be much disappointed if he was

not in at the death. They slowed up and soon the young hunter came in sight.

"Did the elk get away?" he demanded.

"No, he is just ahead," answered Dave. "Don't you hear him?"

"Sure enough. So you waited for me? I'm glad you did."

Away they went in a bunch, until the elk could be heard less than five rods away. Then came a silence.

"He has turned and is going to fight," cried Barringford, and a moment later they came in sight of the elk, backed up against a clump of walnuts, standing at bay, with dilated nostrils and a gaze of mingled alarm and rage in his large, round eyes.

"He is your game, Henry," said Barringford, and Henry took aim promptly at one of those eyes. The elk made a rush, but he was too late. Bang! went Henry's gun. The game gave a wild leap,—and fell dead in his tracks.

Edward Stratemeyer

CHAPTER VI

SURRENDER OF FORT DETROIT

"A good shot!" cried Dave, as all of the party moved forward to inspect the dead elk.

"Couldn't have been better nohow," came from Sam Barringford. He looked the game over carefully. "About as large as I've seen in these parts," he added.

"He has got just the kind of horns I've been wanting to get," said Henry, with pardonable pride. "But I reckon either of you could have hit him in the eye, too," he added candidly.

"It is going to be no easy job getting him home," said Dave. "Shall we put him on a drag?"

"Yes, lad, an' I've a rope we can slip over those horns, an' all can take hold," said Barringford. "We can go as far as possible by the river; for that will be easier."

Barringford carried a sharp hatchet in his belt and with this he cut down a suitable tree branch and fashioned it into such a drag as was desired. Then the elk was lifted upon it and bound fast, and the rope was fastened to the horns.

Getting through the forest to the river was no mean task,

but once on the ice progress was rapid, and long before nightfall they were within easy walking distance of home.

"Game here is not near as plentiful as it was three or four years ago," remarked Dave as they pushed on. "Don't you remember how we used to go out, Henry, and bring down all sorts of small animals?"

"Some day there won't be anything left," put in Barringford. "Time was when buffalo were plentiful, but now you've got to go a long distance to spot 'em. How this elk got here is a mystery to me. I thought they stayed up near the lakes."

"The heavy winter made him go a long distance for food, I reckon," answered Henry; and this was probably the correct explanation.

Little Nell was at the window, arranging a row of pegs Rodney had made for her in the form of a company of soldiers. The largest peg went for the captain, and this she called Washington, while another, which would not stand, but insisted upon falling over, she called General Braddock, for she had heard the older folks talk over Braddock's fearful defeat at Fort Duquesne and of what Washington had done to save what was left of the English troops from annihilation.

"Here they come!" shouted the little miss. "And, oh, such a big deer as they have!"

"An elk, as sure as fate!" ejaculated Rodney, looking over her shoulder. "Henry will have the horns he wanted now."

"And we need the meat," said James Morris, as he flung open the door and hurried outside. "Elk is pretty strong, I know, but it is better than no fresh meat at all. And I am tired of rabbit."

The party of hunters soon came up, and all of the others, including Mrs. Morris, surveyed the game with interest, while they listened to how the elk had been tracked and brought low.

"Certainly worth going many miles for," said James Morris. "The pelt is a fine one."

The elk was hung up out of the reach of any wild beasts that might be prowling around, and the next day Henry and Sam Barringford skinned the animal and cut up the meat as Mrs. Morris desired it. The tongue was smoked, a small part of the forequarter pickled, and the remainder kept fresh by being hung up where it was cold. That day they dined on elk steaks and all pronounced the fresh meat very acceptable.

Late in the afternoon Paul Thompson came to the cabin on horseback, bringing his wife with him.

"We were coming sooner," said the husband, "but my wife got a sore throat and I thought I had better wait until she was well again."

"I hope it is all right now," replied Mrs. Morris, as she escorted her visitors into the cabin.

"Quite well, but she mustn't expose herself too much. When I go to Dennett's I am going to get her a mixture from the doctor."

The Thompsons were astonished to see the babies and wanted at once to hear all about them.

"It certainly is a queer mix-up,' said the man, later on. "I'll see if I can learn anything about them when I am away. Somebody ought to be able to place them,—although, to be sure, a great number of children have become hopelessly lost during the late war."

"We know that," answered Mrs. Morris with a shudder. "Wasn't little Nell stolen from us by the Indians and then held by that bad French trader, Jean Bevoir?"

"Didn't you say Bevoir was dead?" asked Paul Thompson.

"He is," answered James Morris, "and I must confess I am rather glad of it. He caused me a great deal of trouble, in one way and another."

"I have news that Fort Detroit has surrendered to us," went on Paul Thompson. "The surrender took place on November the twenty-ninth,"

"Is that so," cried Dave, with deep interest. "Was there any fighting?"

"I don't believe there was, but the French commander was very bitter over the surrender, and so was Pontiac, the chief of the Ottawas."

"Pontiac?" repeated Henry. "I don't know that I ever heard of him."

"I have," put in Dave. "Somebody told me he was with the Indians that attacked General Braddock, at the opening of the war."

"Yes, he was thar," came from Barringford. "An' I heard tell at thet hospital I was in up to Canada thet he was with Montcalm when the French fit General Wolfe. Montcalm give him a suit of French officer's clothes and the Injun was tickled to death over 'em."

The news that Fort Detroit had surrendered to the English was true. Immediately after the fall of Montreal, as already described in detail in this series, General Amherst ordered Major Robert Rogers, of Rogers' Rangers fame, to ascend the St. Lawrence and the Great Lakes, and take possession of Detroit, Michillimackinac—now called Mackinaw—and other French strongholds which had not yet been turned over to the British.

The start was made on the twelfth of September, 1760, and the force under Rogers consisted of two hundred men, a mere handful as troops as reckoned to-day, but one which was considered amply large enough to accomplish its purpose. The journey was made in a dozen or more whaleboats, and Fort Niagara was reached on the first of October,—about the time Dave, Henry, and Barringford received their release from the army and prepared to start for the Morris home hundreds of miles away.

Moving up the Niagara River as far as the rapids, Rogers' force carried their boats with their loads around the Falls, and then embarked for the journey up Lake Erie, stopping at the fort at Presqu' Isle, and at several other points.

Winter was now on in all its fury, and a heavy rain made Rogers go into camp in the forest bordering the water. Hardly had this been done when a number of Indians put in an appearance and demanded to know where the English soldiers were going.

"This is French and Indian territory," said they. "You can advance no further."

Rogers tried to explain that the war was now over and that all the land belonged to England. But the Indians would not listen, and said he must wait until they had consulted the great chief Pontiac.

When Pontiac finally came, dressed as became a great warrior, he listened gravely to what Rogers had to say. He was much chagrined to learn that the French had capitulated and said that he must have the night in which to think it over. When he went away Rogers and his soldiers feared treachery, but it did not come.

The next day Pontiac came once more. He now said he was willing to let the English advance, provided they would do what was right by his followers and treat him as his rank deserved. Rogers said he would do the best he could; and both smoked the pipe of peace.

When the mouth of the Detroit River was gained word came in that a large body of Indians was hiding in the forest bordering the stream, waiting to slaughter the whites. At once the rangers were on the alert, but the threatened attack did not come, for Pontiac told the Indians that it would be useless to fight the English at present, that they might rather become friends with them and await the settlement of the war between England and France.

Captain Beletre was in command at Fort Detroit. When the news was first brought to him that the French at Montreal had surrendered he refused to believe it.

"I will fight!" he cried, and did his best to arouse the Indians to aid him in defeating the object of Rogers' mission. But when the Colonial commander sent him a copy of the terms of the capitulation Beletre was forced to submit, and did so with the best grace possible. Soon the *fleur de lis* of France was lowered and the cross of St. George of England floated proudly from the flagstaff.

Edward Stratemeyer

This surrender without bloodshed caused great wonder among the red men, and their wonder increased when they saw the French made prisoners with no attempt on the part of the rangers to massacre them. They thought that the English must indeed be powerful, and were glad that they had taken Pontiac's advice and remained, for the time being, friendly.

Detroit taken,—it was at that time but a straggling village with a rude palisade,—a detachment was sent to the south, to occupy Fort Miami and Fort Ouatanon, places of lesser importance. Then Rogers himself set out up Lake Huron to take Michillimackinac. But winter was now on in all its severity, and his boats were driven back by the snow and floating ice, so that he had to abandon this portion of his task. But it may be mentioned here that during the following spring, now so close at hand, a body of Royal Americans journeyed to Michillimackinac and took possession. Thus was the surrender of the French in America made complete so far as it embraced the territory which had been in dispute for so many years. The English imagined that times of peace and plenty were to follow. But they had not reckoned with Pontiac or with the thousands of Indians who stood ready to dig up the war hatchet at the call of this daring and learned chief.

CHAPTER VII

PREPARING FOR THE EXPEDITION WESTWARD

The winter had been a severe one, but early in March came a rapid change and in a few days the spring thaw began in earnest, flooding the banks of the creeks and rivers and causing not a little damage to such buildings as were located close to the water's edge. The forest in that vicinity was still heavy, so that the freshet was not as severe as it is in these days, when there remains but little timber to break the rush of snow and ice and water down the sides of hills and mountains.

With the coming of spring James Morris began to make his arrangements for visiting his trading-post on the Kinotah. In the meantime those at the cabin did their best to learn something concerning the two babies Sam Barringford had picked up. But the efforts in this direction were without success.

Nothing could be learned of the traveler who had the little children, although diligent inquiries were pursued at Fort Bedford, and many other points. Letters were sent to Annapolis and to Philadelphia concerning Barringford's discovery but brought no satisfaction. Once a party wrote that the children might belong to his dead brother, but this proved to be untrue.

Edward Stratemeyer

"It's a complete mystery, that's what it is," declared Henry.

"And it looks to me as if it will never be solved," added Dave.

The children still remained at the Morris house and Mrs. Morris gave both the best of care. The kind woman felt positive that they were twins, and all who saw the children agreed that she was right. One was slightly darker than the other in eyes and hair, and one chin was rounder than the other, but otherwise it was next to impossible to tell them apart.

"Reckon I'll have to shoulder 'em as my own," remarked Sam Barringford one day. "I'd do it in a minit if it wasn't thet I haven't nary a home to take 'em to."

"You may leave them here," said Mrs. Morris promptly. "I have talked it over with Joseph and with James and it will be quite suitable."

"If you'll take 'em in charge I'll pay you for it, Mistress Morris," said the old frontiersman. "It will be a weight off my shoulders to have ye do it. I know as how the little chaps will get the best o' care."

And so it was arranged that the twins should remain with Mrs. Morris. Barringford named them Tom and Artie, after two uncles of his own, and these names clung to them as they grew older. Little did Barringford or the Morrises dream of what the finding of these twins was to lead to in years to come.

"Of one thing I am certain," said James Morris one day. "They are of good breeding. No common blood flows in their veins."

"I take it you are right," answered his brother. "And it may be that some day Sam will be well rewarded for saving them from death."

After a great deal of deliberation it had been decided that James Morris should start for the west about the first of May. Dave and Henry were to go with him, and likewise Sam Barringford and three other frontiersmen named Lukins, Sanderson, and Jadwin. The party was likewise to contain four Indians of the Delaware tribe under White Buffalo. The whites were all to go mounted and were to take six pack-horses in addition. At first James Morris thought to take a couple of wagons, at least as far as Fort Pitt, but this plan was at the last moment abandoned, for wagons were scarce and high in price, and there was no telling if they could be sold when the last fort on the frontier was gained, and further progress with anything on wheels became out of the question.

The coming of White Buffalo with his handful of trusted braves was an event for Dave and Henry. This chief had been their friend for many years and they felt that they could rely upon him, no matter how great the emergency. In the past the tribe to which White Buffalo belonged had been split, some fighting with the English and others with the French, but now some of the leaders, including Skunk Tail, were dead, and, the war being at an end, all were reunited under the leadership of White Buffalo and a young chief named Rain Cloud. But White Buffalo could not forgive some of the men of his tribe for taking up arms against the English and he was glad enough in consequence to get away with his few chosen ones.

"How? How?" said the Indian, meaning "How do you do?" as he took first Dave's hand and then Henry's and gave each a tight grip. "White Buffalo is glad to see his young friends looking so well. The war has not harmed them."

"No, White Buffalo, we are as well as ever," answered Dave. "And how have you been since last we saw you?"

"White Buffalo is not so young as he once was," answered the chief. "His step is not so light and his eye cannot see so far. Before many winters he will be gathered to his fathers."

"Nonsense!" put in Henry. "You can shoot as straight as any of us, and I know it, and walk just as far, too. Who told you that you couldn't?"

"The young braves at White Buffalo's village. They do not care for a chief who is old."

"They make a big mistake, and I'd tell them so if I had the chance," went on Henry earnestly. "You are all right, White Buffalo, and we'll be very glad to have you along, even if your tribe doesn't want you any longer."

At this the eyes of the old Delaware glistened. "Henry is my true friend," he murmured. "And David is my friend, too. White Buffalo shall never forget them."

"Are the men with you young men?" questioned Dave.

"No, they are almost as old as White Buffalo himself."

"That will suit father. He doesn't care for the young braves. They always want to do what pleases them and not what is ordered."

"They are like untrained dogs, who follow one trail and then another and hunt out nothing," was the old chief's comment.

True to his word, he had brought a new doll for little Nell, made by himself with no other tool than his hunting knife.

It was of wood, with eyes of beads, and with joints fastened with deer thongs. It was wonderfully painted, and on the top of the head was a bit of fur for hair.

"White Buffalo bring the papoose he told of," he said, producing it from under his blanket. "Lady papoose, her name Minnehaha."

"Oh, what a beautiful, beautiful doll!" screamed little Nell, as she embraced it. "And her arms and legs move, too! And such a nice name, Minnehaha."

"What does Minnehaha mean?" asked Mrs. Morris, as she too surveyed the precious gift.

"Minnehaha means Laughing Water," answered the Indian chief. "Grand lady, like Queen."

"She is certainly a grand doll," put in Rodney. "Nell, you must take the best of care of it."

"I shall," answered the little miss; and she did.

James Morris had gone to Annapolis, accompanied by his brother, and at this important seaport purchased such things as were needed for the expedition, including some extra weapons, powder, ball and shot, a box of flints, some clothing, and many other things of more or less usefulness. To these were added, when Will's Creek was again reached, two casks of salt pork, two bags of beans, a sack of flour, a canister of coffee, others of sugar, salt, pepper, and various other articles meant for the table. No fresh meat was taken, the party depending upon their firearms to supply game and their lines and hooks to furnish fish. A small supply of feed was also taken for the horses, but this was to be used only when natural fodder could not be found.

Edward Stratemeyer

And all this was for an expedition from Cumberland to the Ohio River, a distance of not much over a hundred miles, and which to-day can be made in the trains inside of three hours with ease! But the trail the party was to take was all of two hundred miles in length, and fifteen to twenty miles per day was considered good traveling. This shows well the progress made in our country in the past one hundred and forty odd years.

There were not sufficient accommodations at the Morris' cabin for all the whites of the party, and the frontiersmen who were to go with Barringford remained at the fort at Cumberland until the start, while the Indians made themselves at home in the woods. Once White Buffalo was invited to take dinner at the cabin, and did so with his usual reserve, eating the meal in almost total silence, and immediately following with a "smoke of peace" between himself and James and Joseph Morris.

"That Indian is one out of a hundred," remarked Joseph Morris to his brother afterward. "I don't believe in trusting them much, but I would trust White Buffalo."

"That is exactly how I feel about it," was the answer, "and why I was so anxious to have him along. He has proved himself our friend through thick and thin. It is too bad that there are not more of such."

"Perhaps there would be, James, had the Indians been treated fairly from the start. But you know as well as I how the traders have cheated them when driving bargains, and how some have given them too much rum and then literally robbed them."

"Yes, yes, I know, and it is the one black spot on our colonization. There should be a law against it. But even that does not warrant the red men in being so savage as they have at times proved themselves."

"True again; but both the English and the French have been almost equally brutal at times. Look at some of the old frontiersmen—those Barringford has often spoken about. They liked a slaughter as well as the Indians, and did not hesitate to scalp the enemy in the same way."

"Yes; but they learned that from the redskins in the first place."

"That is true, too; but they should not have taken up the custom, but instead they should have tried to teach the Indians to do better," concluded Joseph Morris; and there the unsatisfactory argument rested.

CHAPTER VIII

ON THE OLD BRADDOCK ROAD

As old readers of this series will remember, there were but two roads or trails leading from the eastward to Fort Pitt, at the junction of the Allegheny and Monongahela rivers, where is to-day located the great manufacturing city of Pittsburg.

The southern road was that cut through at the time General Braddock made his unsuccessful attack on Fort Duquesne, as the stronghold was then named by the French. This ran through Great Meadows and then northward to Fort Pitt. It started at Fort Cumberland, and passed within short walking distance of where the Morris homestead was located.

The northern road was that cut through by General Forbes during the second campaign against Fort Duquesne, when the French had been driven from that territory by the English troops and Royal Americans. This started from Fort Bedford, about thirty miles north of Fort Cumberland, and ran over the Allegheny Mountains, and across Stony Creek, Bushy Run, and oilier streams. It was a considerably shorter route than the other, but the trail was, in certain spots, more difficult.

At first James Morris, had thought to use the upper and shorter route, but he was fairly well acquainted with the other, and at last decided to stick to that which he knew rather than experiment with the unknown.

"I know we can get through on General Braddock's road," he said. "It may take a few days longer, but time is of no immense value to us."

"You are quite sure the Indians on that road are at peace with us?" asked his brother's wife timidly, "I do not wish Henry to get into more fighting. He saw quite enough of that during the war."

"White Buffalo assures me that, for the present, the war hatchet has been buried everywhere, Lucy. To be sure, there is no telling when it will be dug up again. But I reckon we can take care of ourselves should trouble come."

The starting of the expedition proved quite an event at Will's Creek, and many neighbors living within a radius of two and three miles came to see them off. Among the number was Paul Thompson, who said he would do what he could for those left behind during the absence of James Morris, Dave, and Henry.

It was a perfect day, with a warm breeze blowing up from the Potomac River. Not a cloud ruffled the sky, and the spring birds filled the air with their melody.

"Puts me in mind of the time I went out to the trading-post with you," said Dave to Sam Barringford, as the two rode along side by side, "Don't you remember what a time we had getting through, and how I fell into the river and was afraid of being captured by the Indians?"

"Yes, lad, I remember it well," answered the old

frontiersman. "But the trail ain't half as bad as it was then— Braddock's pioneers smoothed down the rough places putty well,—not but what some of the brushwood has grown up ag'in."

"Shall we stop again at the Indian village of Nancoke?"

"The village ain't thar no more, Dave; fire in the forest swept it away last year, so I heard tell some time ago. But I reckon we'll stop at some redskin village afore we git to the Kinotah."

The end of the first day's traveling found the party miles beyond the last plantation on the road. They stopped in the midst of a little clearing where there had once been a house, but this the Indians had burnt years before and the tall brushwood covered the half-burnt logs and choked up the neighboring spring.

"The trail is poor," observed James Morris. "Much poorer than I expected. We shall have our own troubles getting through."

"It is not as good as when Barringford and I marched under General Braddock," answered Dave. "Then the pioneer corps cut down every tree and bush that was in our way."

"And lost so much time our army was defeated," put in the old frontiersman grimly. "Braddock meant well, but he didn't know how to fight Indians."

Early in the morning the movement forward was resumed. There was a small stream to cross, and a long hill, and then they entered into the depths of a primeval forest, where the tops of the trees were a hundred feet and more overhead, and the great twisted roots lay sprawling in all directions, covered partly with moss and decayed leaves. The trail was still visible, but the branches of the trees on either side met overhead, cutting off the sunlight and making it uncomfortably dark excepting at midday.

James Morris and Sam Barringford led the way, with the frontiersmen, Lukins, Sanderson, and Jadwin, bringing up on either side. Back of these came the pack-horses with their loads, looked after by Dave and Henry, and further to the rear were the Indians under White Buffalo. All told the party made quite an imposing appearance, and if put to it could have offered considerable opposition to any enemy that might have appeared.

The route through the forest soon grew worse. The heavy frost of the past winter had upheaved many rocks and they lay scattered in all directions on the side of a hill up which they were climbing. Sometimes a horse would slip on them and go down, and once a pack animal rolled completely over, smashing flat what was on his back.

"There goes our beans!" cried Henry. "Oh, what luck!"

Dave gave a look, and then, regardless of the seriousness of the situation, burst into a laugh. The beans were rolling in all directions, under the rocks and the horses' feet. It took some time to rescue the fallen animal and gather up the best part of the beans.

"Never mind," said Barringford philosophically. "Those beans will grow, and when you come back this way ag'in ye can pick 'em, Henry."

"Thank you, but I shan't come back just for a quart or two of beans," was the youth's answer. If the silence was sometimes oppressive during the day it was doubly so at night. Occasionally some birds would break the stillness, or they would hear the croaking of frogs in the marshes, or the bark of a distant fox, but that was all. If any big game was at hand it took good care to keep its distance.

The party soon reached the river where Dave had had his stirring adventure on horseback, as already described in "With Washington in the West," and the youth pointed out to his cousin the spot where he had gone into the rapids.

"I'll never forget that event," said he, with something like a shudder. "It was what Barringford would call a close call."

Fortunately there was now a good fording place at hand, so the entire party crossed without difficulty. On the other shore the trail made a new turn, and now began the ascent of a long hill, up which the pack-horses moved with the pace of snails. Those in the saddle had often to dismount and lead their steeds, and at the end of each mile all stopped for a needed rest.

"Don't know as this 'ere trail is as good as tudder," remarked Sam Barringford. "But they tell me it knocks three miles out o' the bend, an' that's something'."

James Morris and the old frontiersman had imagined the weather would remain fair, but on the morning of the fourth day out a cold rain set in that chilled all to the bone. The Indians under White Buffalo wished to go into camp at once, but James Morris decided to keep on and did so until the middle of the afternoon, when, as the storm increased, the party halted beneath a large clump of trees and lost no time in getting out their shelters and putting them up. The Indians had a wigwam of skins and the whites two canvas coverings. These were placed close together, and a roaring camp fire was started near by, where all hands tried to dry themselves and get warm. A steaming hot meal was also served, which did much to make everybody feel comfortable.

"I do hate a cold rain on a march," grumbled Henry, as he crouched in the shelter beside Dave. "Makes me feel like a wet hen that can't get inside of the coop."

"If only one doesn't catch cold," replied Dave. "Don't you remember the cold I caught when we were up at Lake Ontario?"

"To be sure; and I had a cold myself." Henry paused for a moment. "Where has Barringford gone?"

"He said he was going to try to stir up some game. I don't know what he expects to get in this rain."

"He ought to know what he is doing. He is the best white hunter that I ever ran across."

An hour passed, and by that time it was dark. The Indians sat in their wigwam smoking and talking in low guttural tones. The white hunters were also telling yarns of the war and of the various Indian uprisings before that time. They were thrilling tales and the youths listened to them with deep interest. Both Dave and Henry had been through a great deal themselves, so they knew that the stories, though wild and wonderful, were probably based on facts. To-day, when we live in such security and comfort, we can hardly realize the dangers and privations those pioneers endured to make our glorious country so full of rich blessings to us.

Growing tired of sitting down, Henry had just arisen to stretch his limbs, when a sudden rushing sound through the forest reached his ears.

"What is that?" he questioned, and instinctively reached for his rifle.

"Some animal, I reckon," answered Dave.

A rifle shot rang out, and the sound came closer. Then, as Henry ran out of the shelter, he uttered a yell of alarm.

"A buffalo! Lookout!"

He was right, a magnificent specimen of the buffalo tribe was crashing along under the wet trees and among the bushes. He was alone and rushing along at his best speed. In a twinkling he struck the clump of trees, and, hitting the shelter of the whites, smashed it flat!

CHAPTER IX

HENRY'S STRANGE DISAPPEARANCE

In days gone by the American buffalo, or bison, roamed nearly the entire length and breadth of North America. The Indians hunted the animal industriously, but their efforts with bow and spear were not sufficient to exterminate the species.

But with the coming of the white man to America matters took a different turn. The buffalo could not run away so easily from a rifle shot, and armed with the best weapons they could obtain, Indians and white hunters rounded up the buffaloes at every possible opportunity, in order to obtain the pelts. This soon caused the animals to thin out and flee to the westward, beyond the Mississippi, where they at last sought refuge in the Rocky Mountains. So fiercely have they been hunted during the past seventy-five years that to-day but a few herds remain and ere long these promise to be totally exterminated.

Henry had never seen a buffalo so far to the eastward and he was therefore much astonished at the sudden appearance of the shaggy-headed beast. He gave a yell of alarm, which was followed by another yell from Dave, as the frail shelter bent beneath the weight of the buffalo.

Edward Stratemeyer

"A bison!" shouted James Morris, and White Buffalo took up the cry of alarm. Then down went the canvas flat, and the buffalo made a plunge for the forest beyond. Henry heard a groan from Dave, as the youth was covered up. Not waiting longer, he raised his gun, took hasty aim at the animal and fired.

"Did ye git him?" The query came from Sam Barringford, as, bare-headed, he rushed into the little clearing back of the trees. "I give him one in the side but it didn't seem to stop him none."

"I don't know if I hit him or not," answered Henry. "He burst upon us so swiftly I hardly knew what to do."

While this talk was going on James Morris was crawling from under the wreck of the tent. Barringford reloaded and ran on after the buffalo and Henry did likewise. They could hear the great beast plunging headlong through the brush.

"He has got it putty bad," remarked Barringford. "If he hadn't he wouldn't ram into things so hard. Reckon he hardly knows what he is doin'."

"I hope we get him," answered Henry, his eyes filled with eager desire. "We would have fresh meat for a long time, and plenty of jerked beef, too."

More than half a mile was covered and still the buffalo kept on, much to the surprise of the young hunter and the pioneer.

"Not so badly hit as I reckoned on," panted Barringford.

"Perhaps I didn't hit him at all," was Henry's answer.

Soon they gained the top of a rise of ground. Here the rocks were smooth and slippery, and in a twinkling Henry went down and rolled over and over down a long hill.

"Hi! hi! stop yourself!" roared Barringford in quick alarm. "Stop, or ye'll go over the cliff!"

His alarm was justified, for the hill ended in a cliff all of thirty feet in height, below which were some jagged rocks and a small mountain torrent flowing into the upper Monongahela.

Henry heard the cry but did not understand the words. Yet he did not like the idea of rolling he knew not to where, and dropping his gun he caught at the wet rocks and bushes which came to hand. But his downward progress was not stayed, and in a few seconds he reached the edge of the cliff and rolled out of sight!

The incident happened so quickly that Barringford was almost stunned. He started to go down the hill after Henry but for fear of meeting a like fate, dropped on his breast in the wet and worked his way along from rock to bush with great caution. Twice he called Henry's name, but no answer came back.

"If he went over on them rocks it's likely he was smashed up," he groaned. "Why didn't I have sense enough to hold him back? I knew this dangerous spot was here."

Step by step he drew closer to the edge of the cliff. The snows of the past winter had washed away and loosened much of the ground, and once he felt as if everything was giving way and he was to share the fate of his companion.

At last he was within three feet of the edge of the cliff. He could look down into the gully beyond but not down on the side where he felt Henry must be resting.

Edward Stratemeyer

"Henry!" he called loudly. "Henry!"

He waited for fully a minute, but no answer came back. His face grew more disturbed than ever.

"He is hurt, that's sartin," he muttered. "Like as not he broke his neck."

Barringford always carried a bit of rope with him and he now had the same piece used in dragging the elk to the Morris homestead. Taking this, he tied it to a stout bush, and by this means lowered himself to the very edge of the cliff.

Night was now approaching, and at the bottom of the gully all was so dark he could see only with the greatest of difficulty. The torrent ran among rough rocks and brush-wood, with here and there a patch of long grass bent flat from the winter's snows.

"Henry! Where are you?"

Again there was no answer, and now Barringford was thoroughly alarmed. He remembered how Mrs. Morris had asked him to keep watch over her son.

"Got to git down to him somehow," he told himself. "I hope he's only stunned."

After a general survey of the situation, the old frontiersman decided that the cliff terminated at a point several hundred yards to the southward. Accordingly, he climbed up the hill with care and commenced to make a detour in that direction.

It was hard work to make any movement forward, for the rocks were unusually rough and between them were hollows filled with mud, dead leaves and water. Three times he fell and when he arose he was plastered with mud from head to feet. But he did not turn back, and every minute wasted only added to his alarm, for Sam Barringford, rough though he was in outward appearance, had a heart that at times could be as tender as that of a child.

"If the lad's dead I don't know how I'm a-goin' to break the news to his folks," he groaned, with a long sigh. "Joseph and his wife allers looked to me to keep an eye on him. They expect me to be keerful. 'Twasn't right at all fer me to take Henry so close to sech a dangerous spot. I ought to be licked fer it, an' licked hard, too."

It was a good half hour before he could get down to where the torrent flowed over the rocks. He was now a quarter of a mile from where Henry had taken the unexpected tumble, and working his way down the stream was no easy task.

It had set in to rain harder than ever, and the black clouds soon shut out what little was left of daylight. Wet to the skin, and shivering from the cold, he moved on as well as he was able. Again he called Henry's name, but only a dull echo came back, partly drowned by the rushing of the water.

When Barringford thought he had covered the proper distance he came to a halt. On his back he carried Henry's rifle as well as his own, having picked it up when leaving the top of the hill, but the owner of the firearm was nowhere visible.

"I'll have to make a light, no two ways on thet," he mused, and moved close up under the rocks to get some dry kindlings. But everything was thoroughly wet around him and though he set fire to the tinder in his box he could obtain nothing in the shape of a torch.

Again he stumbled on, soon getting into the water up to his waist. In fresh alarm he found his way out of the torrent and next encountered some thick, wiry bushes where further progress seemed out of the question.

"Beats all, how things are goin' crosswise," he muttered, as he paused to get his breath. "An' all along o' thet confounded buffalo, too. Reckon he's miles an' miles away by this time," and in this surmise the old frontiersman was correct.

An hour's search convinced him that Henry was no longer in that vicinity. But what had become of the youth was a mystery.

"He wouldn't walk away without lettin' me know," reasoned Barringford. "Must be he fell into the water and got drowned and somethin' is holdin' him under. One thing is sartin, if thet's so tain't no use to try to find him afore mornin'. Might as well go back to camp an' break the news."

But he was unwilling to go back, and again and again he called Henry's name, listening with all the acuteness of which his trained sense of hearing was capable. Only the rushing of the torrent and the dripping of the rain answered him.

"No use," he muttered. "He is gone an' thet is all there is to it. I've got to face the music and tell the others, though it's worse nor pullin' teeth to do it."

Getting out of the gully in the almost total darkness was now truly difficult, and had not Barringford been skilled in woodcraft he would certainly have been lost. But he had taken note of the way he had come and remembered every bush, tree, and rock, and now he returned by the same route. It was a tough climb back to the forest where the trail of the buffalo had been last seen and here he had to rest once more, before starting for the camp.

Edward Stratemeyer

CHAPTER X

A WAIT IN CAMP

Let us go back to the time when the buffalo, in his mad eagerness to get away from the hunters, plunged headlong into the shelter of the whites and hurled it flat.

Under the canvas lay Dave, with the breath knocked completely out of him. He felt something heavy come down on his back and then for the moment knew no more.

When he opened his eyes he found that his father had hauled him from under the wreckage and was gazing earnestly into his face.

"Are you hurt, son?" demanded James Morris quickly.

"I—I—reckon not" was the slow answer. "But something hit me in the—the back. Whe—where is the buffalo?"

"Gone, and Barringford and Henry after him."

"Hope they lay him low."

"So do I. But are you quite sure you are not injured? I thought the animal stepped on you."

"Maybe he did, father. But I'm all right, thank goodness." And Dave stretched himself to prove his words.

The Indians had gathered around and were talking excitedly. Some wanted to join in the hunt, but the frontiersmen under Barringford held them back.

"You let Sam an' Henry go it alone," said Sanderson. "They know wot they are a-doin'."

"That is true," answered White Buffalo. "My white brothers can shoot well—I have seen it."

Soon the knocked-down tent was raised again, and the fire stirred up. Then, as the storm, increased, all crouched in the shelters they had erected and awaited the return of Henry and the old frontiersman.

"I'd like to eat a buffalo steak now first-rate," said Dave, smacking his lips. "It would touch the spot and chase away the blues."

"Buffalo steak is rather strong, like elk's meat," answered his father. "But we need strong food, on such a rough journey as this."

"It's a pity there isn't a better trail, father."

"Some day there will be a regular road, Dave—when there are more settlements to the westward. I look for the time when we shall have cities out here, the same as along the seaboard."

"Won't never see that" said the frontiersman named Lukins.

"Why not?" risked James Morris.

Edward Stratemeyer

"The Injuns won't allow it, that's why, Mr. Morris. They don't mind a tradin'-post or two, whar they kin sell hides an' git rum an' sech things. But they don't want no towns or cities. You won't never see a city on the Ohio, nor in them Western countries at all."

"I believe the cities are bound to come," said Dave. "As more folks come over from England, and Germany, and France, they'll be bound to spread out. The Indians won't stop 'em."

"They will if they rise an' dig up the war hatchet," put in Jadwin, the other frontiersman.

"If they dig up the hatchet too often they will be wiped out," said James Morris. "They may fight all they please—in the end both the English and the French will conquer them."

"How large do you think our country will get in time, father?" questioned Dave.

"That is a hard question to answer, Dave. I think you may live to see strong settlements on the Ohio, and your children may see towns on the Mississippi. About the great Western countries I know nothing, nor does any other white man. I suppose they are overrun by Indians and all sorts of wild beasts, or perhaps there is nothing there but beasts and trackless forests."

"It's too bad the Indians won't live as the white people live," went on Dave thoughtfully. "We might get along famously together."

"It is not the Indian's nature to till the soil, my son. He loves to roam about and to hunt and fish and then take it easy. More than this, when the spirit stirs him, he must fight; and if he cannot fight the white man he will fight his fellow Indians. You have often heard White Buffalo tell how one tribe will fight another tribe for several seasons, and how the tribes sometimes split up and fight among themselves."

"Of course; didn't the Delawares to whom he belongs split up, one side going to the French and the others fighting under White Buffalo for our cause? But when a war is over they might settle down."

As the time passed the others concluded that Henry and Barringford had found the buffalo hunt longer than they had anticipated.

"Perhaps the animal has led them such a chase they won't come back until morning," suggested James Morris. "It is no fine thing to travel in the wet and darkness."

"Right you are," said Sanderson. "Sam may hunt in the wet if he wants to, but none of it for me."

An early supper was had, and something was kept hot for those who were missing, for it was felt they would come in chilled to the bone and with tremendous appetites.

Dave was beginning to grow sleepy when he heard a movement outside, and a moment later Sam Barringford came into view, with downcast face and with the water dripping from his coonskin cap and hunting shirt.

"Sam!" cried James Morris, leaping up. "So you've got back at last. Did you get the buffalo? Where is Henry?"

"No, we didn't get the buffalo," answered the old frontiersman. His voice grew husky. "Henry—he is—missing—he dropped over a cliff—" He could not go on.

"Over a cliff!" gasped Dave. "You don't mean he is—is—"
He too failed to finish what was in his mind.

"I can't tell you what happened after he slipped from my
sight," went on Barringford.

"Oh, Sam, do you mean to say he is killed?"

"I hope not, lad. But it looks juberous, no two ways on't."

"Tell me how it happened," said James Morris, and now all
in the camp gathered around to hear what the old
frontiersman had to say.

The ice once broken, Barringford's tongue grew more
talkative, and he related all the particulars so far as he knew
them.

"When I worked my way down into the waterway I felt
sartin I would find Henry in some sort o' shape," he
concluded. "But I couldn't find nuthin', not even his cap.
His gun he dropped on the hill, an' here it is," and he
handed it to Dave.

It was a fearful shock, and the tears stood in Dave's eyes and
ran down his cheeks, while the youth's father was scarcely
less affected. The frontiersmen had little to say, and the
Indians, with the exception of White Buffalo, took the
matter stoically, for the perils of the hunt were no new
things to them.

White Buffalo took in every word that was spoken. When
matters of importance were to be considered he had little to
say.

"Shall White Buffalo go forward and make a search?" he
asked simply, after Sam Barringford had stopped speaking.

"What can you do, after Sam here has failed?" questioned James Morris. "I know you are keen on the trail, White Buffalo, but you know that Sam is too."

"Four eyes are better than two," returned the Indian, using an old saying of his tribe.

"Let him go by all means if he wishes," put in Barringford. "The man to find Henry an' bring him back to camp is my best friend."

"White Buffalo, will you take me along?" asked Dave eagerly.

"Dave, son, don't you think you had better remain with me?" asked his father.

"No, father; we must find Henry. Please let me go!"

"Dave can go if he wishes," answered White Buffalo. "The journey will not be pleasant, but if Henry is found we shall be glad. Is not White Buffalo right?"

"Take torches with you, or a lantern," said Barringford.

Torches were quickly procured and placed in a bit of skin, that they might not get wet. Then another torch was lit, and the old frontiersman gave the Indian chief minute directions about the trail to the water course under the cliff.

"White Buffalo knows something of that land," said the chief. "He will not go astray."

"I should hope not," said Dave. "We want to find Henry, not lose ourselves."

"Take a bag full of eating along," put in James Morris. "You may want something before morning. And also a bandage and some stimulants for Henry, in case he is badly hurt and needs them." He could not let himself believe that his nephew was dead.

"All right, father; I'll take whatever you say," answered Dave, and soon he and White Buffalo had all the articles mentioned. Each went armed with his rifle and hunting knife, and the Indian carried his hatchet as well.

"Do not remain away later than to-morrow noon," said James Morris, when they were ready to leave. "If you are not back by that time I shall fear that something has happened to you also."

"Don't fear for me so long as I am with White Buffalo," replied Dave; and this speech pleased the Indian chief very much.

"Don't you try to go down to the stream by way of the hill," cautioned Sam Barringford. "If you do you may break your necks."

The old frontiersman had sprained his foot, but he did not deem it best to mention that fact. Nevertheless, if he had been better able to walk he would probably have accompanied Dave and White Buffalo in spite of the first search made by him.

"It's a shame, thet's wot it is," he declared, after the youth and the Indian had departed. "It distresses me oncommonly to think such a thing could happen to Henry."

"I hope with all my heart he is alive," responded James Morris.

"But if he is dead—?"

"Then I shall return to Will's Creek without delay, and start for the west some time later—after I have given my brother and his family all the comfort I can," said the trader soberly.

CHAPTER XI

HAPPENINGS OF A STORMY NIGHT

It is now high time that we return to Henry and see how he fared after his sudden and unexpected disappearance over the edge of the cliff.

The young pioneer was well aware of his peril and as he rolled out of Sam Barringford's sight he clutched wildly at every bush and projecting rock that came near his hand.

Once a sapling, growing in a cleft of the cliff, struck his shoulder. Around this he managed partly to twist his arm, and this saved him from serious injury.

He struck some rocks, however, with considerable force and for a moment was stunned.

"What a tumble!" he muttered, when he had regained his breath. "It is a wonder that I didn't kill myself,"

With an ache in the side occasioned by the rough experience, Henry arose and started to look for some spot along the cliff where he might climb to the top.

Where he stood it was almost totally dark, and he had not taken over a score of steps when he floundered into a hollow filled with water and mud. He leaped across this, to find himself in a split of the cliff, where the bushes were unusually high and thick. Here the rain hung heavily from every twig and soon soaked him worse than ever.

He thought he heard Barringford calling and started to answer. Then he pushed forward once more, hoping each moment to gain higher ground.

But the pocket,—for such it really was,—grew deeper, and suddenly he found himself at the edge of a deep hole. He tried to step back, but the dirt under his feet gave way and he plunged downward he knew not whither. He felt his head strike some projection, and felt some dirt come down on top of him, and then, for the time being, he knew no more.

The young hunter came to his senses slowly. His first realization was that his head pained him greatly, and that some weight was trying to force the air from his lungs. He tried to move his hands, to learn that each was covered with the dirt which had come down on top of him.

With a great effort he cleared his hands and then his body and tried to rise to his feet. But he could not stand, and trembling like a leaf he sank down on a rock near at hand. All was pitch dark around him and the rain beat steadily on his head.

"I'm in a pickle truly!" he muttered dismally. "Wonder where Sam can be?"

He tried to cry out, but his voice was woefully weak and uncertain, and he soon gave up the effort. Then he tried again to walk, but had to desist in despair.

He could not imagine how long he had been under the

fallen dirt, but knew it must be some time, perhaps an hour or two. Where Barringford was there was no telling.

"I'm worse off than I was before, that is sure," he thought. "Maybe I won't be able to get out of this mess before morning."

Feeling stronger after a while he arose and groped his way forward. He had not taken a dozen steps before he came to some rocks. They arose slantingly, and under them he found a dry spot, well sheltered from the rain.

"This is a little better than the other place was," he mused. "But I'd like to know just what sort of a hole this is, and what the prospect is of getting out."

Like Barringford, the young pioneer carried a flint and tinder-box with him, and under the rocks it was a comparatively easy matter for Henry to strike a light. He found some dry leaves and twigs, blown hither by the wind, and presently had a respectable fire started, over which he crouched in an effort to drive away the chill which was stealing over him.

"This is a buffalo hunt with a vengeance," he muttered. "I was a fool to start off after the animal in such a storm, and in the darkness. After this, I'll do my hunting altogether in the daytime."

In a search for more firewood Henry presently came to an opening in the rocks behind him. It was totally dry here and, taking up the best of the firebrands, he moved to the new location. Soon he had a roaring fire, the smoke going upward, to some hole overhead which he could not locate.

"This must be something of a cave," he mused. "Wonder where it can lead to."

He felt that it would be useless to attempt trying to get out of the hollow he was in before daylight and so proceeded to make an investigation of the opening.

It proved of no great size, however, and nothing met his gaze but rocks, dirt, decayed tree roots, and a heap of bones in a far corner, showing that it had once been the den of a wild beast.

"I am glad the beast isn't here now," thought Henry. "I'd be badly off without a gun."

Slowly the time wore away and Henry had now to make another search for firewood, if he expected to keep the blaze going, and what to do he scarcely knew.

"If I look for wood I'll get wet again," he reasoned. "And if I don't go and get some the fire will leave me in the cold."

He was on the point of scraping the fire together, to make it last as long as possible, when an unexpected whistle broke upon his ears. He sprang to the front of the shelter and listened intently. The whistle was one he knew well, and the whistler was rendering an old English air, called "Lucy Locket Lost Her Pocket," an air which we to-day call "Yankee Doodle."

"Dave!" shouted the young hunter, and set up a wild yell. "Dave! Where are you?"

"Is that you, Henry?" came from the edge of the hollow.

"Yes. Look out, or you'll get a tumble as I did."

"White Buffalo knows the trail," came in the voice of the Indian chief.

"Hullo! is that you, White Buffalo? Very well, but be careful."

Torches in hand, Dave and White Buffalo moved forward slowly. But the Indian knew exactly what he was doing, and soon he and the youth with him were at the bottom of the hollow in safety. Then Dave ran forward to greet his cousin.

"Are you badly hurt?" he questioned.

"No. I'm all right, Dave, although I got two nasty tumbles."

"Sam was afraid you had been killed. He searched all around, but couldn't find you."

"I was foolish not to wait until Sam came down to the water course. I started to get out alone and got into this pickle. Why didn't you shout when you came up?"

"We saw the fire but White Buffalo thought there might be some unfriendly Indians or trappers around. So then I thought of my old whistle. I knew you would recognize it."

Henry had to tell his story, and then Dave asked him if he was well enough to return to the camp without delay.

"They are all anxious about you, especially father and Sam," he added.

"To be sure, I'll go back to camp. It's no fun staying here. I'm quite hungry, too."

"Then you must have something before we leave."

The meal was soon disposed of, and led by White Buffalo the party left the hollow and proceeded through the forest. It was a long, hard journey, but neither of the youths minded it, both being thankful that the adventure had terminated so happily.

When Henry reached camp once more he was hailed with great joy by James Morris and Sam Barringford. The uncle embraced his nephew, and the old frontiersman gripped Henry's hand until the bones fairly cracked.

"I have been more than worried ever since Sam came back with his sad tale," said James Morris. "In the future, Henry, you must be very careful when you go hunting; otherwise I shall not want to leave you out of my sight."

"I'd give my right hand ruther than see ye kilt," said Barringford huskily. "Next time we go out I reckon as how we'll keep close together."

"It's strange you didn't get on my trail," returned Henry. "You are usually a good one at such things."

"The downpour washed out the tracks," said James Morris.

"I'm not so good at such things as White Buffalo is," answered Sam Barringford bluntly. "He is born to it, and, White Buffalo, it does you credit."

"White Buffalo was once called the Trail King," said the Delaware proudly. "He found the trail when all others failed. It was in the war with the Ottawas."

The rain had now ceased, and once more the camp-fires were started up and the wet things were placed to dry.

"Since so much of the night has been lost we may as well take it easy to-morrow," said James Morris, and this was done. This gave Barringford a chance to nurse his sprained foot, for which he was thankful.

CHAPTER XII

THE RUINS OF THE OLD TRADING-POST

Once more the arduous journey westward was resumed. The hills left behind, they traveled a peaceful valley where riding on horseback was a real pleasure. Small game was now sighted in plenty, and Dave and Henry brought down their full share of what was bagged. The Indians joined in the hunting with keen pleasure, and White Buffalo brought down a silver-tailed fox, the pelt of which became the envy of all the red men under him.

Having crossed a broad but shallow water course, they reached an Indian village called Badoktah, which had but recently been established by a tribe of the Shawanoes. The coming of the Shawanoes eastward into the territory of the Delawares was not liked by the latter, and White Buffalo and his men met those in the village with scant courtesy.

"The land of the Shawanoes is beyond the rolling Muskingum," said White Buffalo to Dave. "They have come hither because they know my tribes are weak. But some day we shall drive them back to the lands that are their own."

"Do they claim the land up at Lake Erie?" asked the youth.

"No, that is the land of the Wyandots and the Iroquois."

"And how far to the west do they own the land?"

"For three days' journey on foot. Then comes the land of the mighty Miamis, and to the northward the lands of the Pottawattamies, the Ottawas, and the Ojibways."

"And who occupy the lands still further westward?"

"On the mighty Father of Waters," answered the Indian chief, meaning the Mississippi, "are the Illinois, and to the northward the Kickapoos and the Sacs and Winnebagoes. Of the tribes beyond the mighty river, White Buffalo knows but little. By some they are said to be exceeding cruel, and others have told that they are dumb and paint their bodies with mud."

The village of Badoktah consisted of about thirty wigwams, made of rude skins and long poles. As was usual at all such villages, each wigwam was decorated with rough Indian pictures and writings, giving the name of the occupant, his family, and telling of his deeds in war. The wigwams were without exception exceedingly dirty, and the Shawanoes themselves were little better—offering a strong contrast to White Buffalo and his followers. Indian dogs were everywhere, many of them miserable curs, all barking viciously, and showing their teeth.

The warriors were getting ready to go out on a hunt, but they waited until their unexpected visitors had departed. One or two of them had met James Morris at the trading-post on the Kinotah, and they remembered that he had treated them well. As a consequence the Indians did what they could to make the newcomers welcome, although they showed plainly that they would have been better pleased had the Delawares not been present.

"You must come and trade with me when I have re-established myself," said James Morris to the warriors of the village. "I will treat you honestly."

They remained in the village but two hours, and then pushed forward straight for Fort Pitt.

At the time of which I write, Fort Pitt was a structure standing on the point of land where the Monongahela and the Alleghany rivers unite to form the broad Ohio. As already told, it had been named Fort Duquesne by the French, but after the surrender to General Forbes, it was re-named after William Pitt, a great leader in England. In 1759, much of the old fort was torn down by General Stanwix, who erected in its place a much larger and stronger structure, built of logs, bricks, and dirt, and well protected with a number of cannon.

When the party reached the fort, James Morris was welcomed warmly by the English officer in command. No white men had passed that way since early winter, and all in the fort were anxious to hear the latest news, and to receive the newspapers which the trader had thoughtfully brought along.

"You are very adventurous," said the commandant of the fort. "I do not know how the Shawanoes will treat you."

"Have you had any trouble?" demanded James Morris.

"Not of any consequence. Some drunken Indians came here a few weeks ago and did some shooting. But nobody was hurt, and I speedily sent the drunkards about their business."

All the whites of the party were glad to rest at the fort for several days, and White Buffalo and his men remained with them. During that time Dave and Henry met several soldiers who had been with the youths during one campaign or another.

"Glad to see you came out of the war hale and hearty," said one of the soldiers. "You are both lucky."

"We were lucky," answered Henry.

"The fall of Montreal has brought the war to a quick close," went on the soldier. "But that is not saying that the Indians won't give us plenty of trouble in the future."

"They had better not. They will get the worst of it," said Dave.

"It is some of the great chiefs who are stirring them up, Morris. If the regular run of redskins were left alone they would be peaceable enough. But the chiefs go among them and say we are stealing their hunting grounds away from them, and all that, and that gets them excited."

"Yes, I know. And, to a certain extent, what they say is true, too."

"The trouble is, the redskins won't make a fair deal. They'll sell land one year and then want it back the next," added another soldier.

"Have you seen any French traders in this vicinity?" asked Henry.

"Not since we gave orders for them to quit their trading. I reckon they feel mighty sore. Our captain told me that a few were thinking of becoming British subjects. They realize that the French hold in America is now broken for good."

The stop at Fort Pitt at an end, the party continued on its way to the Kinotah, a beautiful stream, the name of which has long since been changed. The trail was now exceedingly rough, and so narrow in spots that the pack-horses could scarcely get through. The branches of the trees hung low, so that often all had to move along on foot. The one consolation was that the weather remained fine, so that camping-out at night proved a real pleasure and a rest.

"There are not half the Indians in this neighborhood that there were three and four years ago," remarked James Morris to Barringford. "The war has thinned them out more than I expected."

"I look for big times with game," returned the old frontiersman. "It will be almost like striking a new hunting ground."

Every night a watch was kept for the possible appearance of an enemy, either two-footed or four-footed. But no man came to disturb them, and if any wild beasts were near they kept well out of sight. Once Lukins brought down a small wild-cat, but that was all.

It must be confessed that James Morris was exceedingly anxious to see how the trading-post had fared during his absence, and as soon as the rolling Kinotah was reached, he set off on a gallop along the bank of the stream, followed by Dave and Henry, leaving Barringford to advance more leisurely with the pack-train.

The river, with its clear, sparkling waters, was as beautiful as ever, but while they were still two miles from where the trading-post had been located, they noticed a change in the character of the surroundings. The heavy spring freshets had done their work, and the river banks were torn into numerous gullies and creeks, while the trunks and limbs of great trees lay in all directions. Further still, they came to a long, burnt district, which made the heart of the trader turn sick with dread.

"It is as I feared," he said sadly. "There has been a terrible burn-over here, and the district is no longer what it was."

In less than half an hour's riding over the blackened ground, they came to where the long, comfortable trading-post had been located. Only a pile of ashes, with here and there a burnt log sticking up, marked the spot, and James Morris could scarcely keep back the tears as he surveyed the ruin wrought. Tears came to Dave's eyes, and Henry shook his head.

"We'll have to go further now, won't we, father?" said Dave, after a long spell of silence. "You won't want to build here again."

"No, Dave, I'll not build here. It was a beautiful place, but it seemed fated not to thrive. We must push on to some other territory."

Dismounting, they started to poke among the ruins, thinking they might possibly turn up something of value. While they were at this task Barringford and the others appeared.

"Well, I vum!" cried the old frontiersman. "Ef this ain't jess too naturally bad fer anything! Didn't expect it like this, did ye? An' sech a handsome spot as it was, too!"

"White Buffalo's heart is sad," said the Indian chief. "He feels sore for his brother James. The great forest has fallen, and many will be the summers ere it rises again."

"You are right, White Buffalo," answered the trader. "And

even when it does rise, it will not be as grand as it was before."

The party could not go into camp on the burn-over, so Sanderson took charge of the pack-train and led it along the river, where the waters flowed toward the broad Ohio. In the meantime, the Morrises and Sam Barringford dug over the ashes where the trading-post had stood.

Little of value was found, outside of a rusty pistol, two rusty hunting knives, a bullet mold, a string of wampum, and a few earthen dishes, and an hour later the searchers left the spot.

"It is too bad," said James Morris. "I loved the place dearly. But it may be we shall find another further on that is just as good."

"Let us hope it will be better," said Dave, trying to look on the cheerful side.

"Yes, let us hope it will be better," said Henry; and the others echoed the sentiment.

CHAPTER XIII

BUILDING THE NEW TRADING-POST

Four days later found the entire party encamped on the bank of the Ohio River, about twenty miles from the district which had suffered from the terrible ravages of fire.

They had, indeed, found a spot as beautiful as that which had once chained James Morris to the Kinotah. There was a tiny bluff overlooking the broad stream, and back of this a long, low hill, covered with a forest of exceptionally good timber. Around the hill wound a pleasing brook, gurgling gently in its passage over the stones. The brook was lined with various kinds of bushes and flowering plants, and not far off was a series of rocks, where a spring of pure, cold water gushed forth. The soil along the river bank was rich in the extreme, and James Morris saw at once that anything planted in it would grow with but little care.

"After all, I think we have done well to come thus far," said he to Dave and Henry. "The Ohio is a larger stream than the Kinotah, hence I think the chances to do some trading will be better." And without loss of time he staked out a plot of ground, and, in his own way, proclaimed himself proprietor. He knew that, later on, he would have to prove his claim to the Land Company claiming the whole tract, but he felt that this, with proper influence, would be easy.

Edward Stratemeyer

The Land Companies were glad to have the backing of honest traders, for to survey their possessions and dispose of certain plots was by no means easy.

The spot for the location of the new trading-post having been found, many hard days of toil followed for all of the white men, and for Dave and Henry. The Indians could not be persuaded to work, but spent their time in hunting and fishing, and thus supplied the entire party with food.

The first work was to build a rude, but substantial palisade, of logs about twelve feet long, and sharpened at the upper end. This palisade extended from the river front to where the brook made a turn, almost parallel to the Ohio, with the north side flanked by a small rise of rocks. The gateway was at the south end, ten feet wide, and later on, fitted with a strong pair of gates, secured by a top and a bottom crossbar.

Fortunately, as already stated, good timber was close at hand, and while Dave, Henry, and Sam Barringford cut the logs, the others had the horses haul them to where they were wanted and set them up as desired. James Morris was an old hand at this sort of employment, and so the work went forth rapidly.

"This is really working for a living," said Dave, one day, after having brought down a tall, straight tree, from which, at least, four logs could be cut. "We are truly earning our bread by the sweat of our face.'

"But it's healthy labor, and I don't mind it," answered his cousin.

"Do you really mean that, Henry?" asked Dave, resting for a moment and gazing sharply at the other.

Henry colored slightly. "I suppose you think I'd rather be

out hunting with White Buffalo's crowd," he said slowly.

"Wouldn't you? Tell the plain truth?"

"Perhaps I would. But I don't let myself think about it, Dave. This work has got to be done, and I mean to do my full share of it. I reckon everybody has to do things he don't just like in this life."

"I think you are right there—I know I often have to do 'em."

"And it don't do to growl either. The best thing to do is to pitch in and get through as fast as possible," went on Henry, and then set to chopping with renewed vigor.

"Do you remember the time we first started to chop down trees?" continued Dave. "How our hands got blistered, and how we wouldn't give up because the men were looking on?"

"Indeed I do. What a lot has happened since that time! The war, and our going to Fort Niagara, and then down the Lakes and the St. Lawrence to Quebec and Montreal, and all the fighting! In one way, Dave, we have seen quite something of life."

"So we have. But I want no more war."

"Neither do I," answered Henry. Neither dreamed of the terrors of the Indian uprising, or of the grim horrors of the Revolution which would come later. The molding of this great nation into what it is to-day was to be no easy matter.

Inside of two months the greater part of the work on the palisade was complete. There were many things still to accomplish, but James Morris decided to let these rest until later. He and the others set to work to clear the grounds within, called the stockade, and then a long, low log house was started at one side, and a low storehouse and horse stable at the other.

So far, but few hunters and trappers had appeared to do any trading. Strange as it may seem, the Ohio at this point had but few Indians upon it, the red men confining their operations very largely to the smaller streams. But those who did appear were treated liberally by James Morris, and soon they spread the news, with the result that quite a fair trade was established by the time snow was flying once more.

The white men, and especially Dave and Henry, were glad enough to shift from the outside camp to the log house as soon as one end of the building was completed. All was still in a crude state, but sleeping under any sort of roof was preferable to the open. The entire house could not be completed that season, so only two rooms were made weather proof, one for trading, and the other for living and sleeping purposes.

"Not as nice as at home," observed Dave, as he gazed at the rough logs, filled in with mud, and the dirt flooring. "But it will be warm this winter, and that's something."

It had been decided that Barrington and Henry should return to the Morris homestead before winter set in. They were to take six of the horses, and, if everything went well, were to return to the trading-post as early as possible in the spring, bringing with them a long list of articles wanted by James Morris. Both were now quite anxious to return to the East, Henry to learn how his folks were faring, and Barringford to see the twins and find out if their identity had yet been disclosed.

"If they ain't found out nuthin' about them twins, I'm

going to make 'em my own," said the old frontiersman. "I ain't got no chick nor child, an' I might as well be a-doin' somethin' for somebody in this world."

"But you must leave them at our house," returned Henry. "Mother and little Nell are so attached to them."

The departure of Henry and Barringford was an event, and all quit working to see them off. Dave was sorry to part with his cousin, and wrung his hand several times.

"You take good care of yourself," he said. "Don't tumble over any more cliffs."

"And you take good care of yourself during the winter," returned Henry. "It snows heavily out here, so they tell me. Don't you get lost in a snowstorm, like you did when you and Sam were journeying to Fort Oswego."

Dave and James Morris accompanied the pair as far as the burn-over and then watched them as they disappeared over a distant ridge. As they were lost to sight, the youth could not repress a sigh, which reached his parent's quick ears.

"Sorry to see Henry go, I suppose, Dave."

"Yes, father. We have been together so much, you know. Henry seems like a brother to me."

"I don't doubt it, for he is to me almost like a son. I trust he and Sam reach Will's Creek in safety."

Both father and son had thought to return to the new trading post as soon as they left the others, but now neither was in the humor for working, for what little was left of the day, and James Morris asked Dave if he wished to go on a short hunt.

Edward Stratemeyer

"We may not stir up much, but I think the change will do us good."

"I'll go gladly!" cried Dave, and they set off on horseback, up the Kinotah, and then followed a small creek, along which both had hunted in days gone by.

The day was an ideal one, and though game in that vicinity was scarce, the Indians having gone over the ground half a dozen times, each enjoyed the outing thoroughly. Dave managed to bring down some birds and two squirrels, and his father a pair of grouse, and with this they rested content.

"Supposing we take another look at the ruins of the old post?" suggested Dave, when they were on the return. "It is not so very late yet, and we may pick up something which we missed before."

"Very well, Dave."

Along the creek the wild flowers grew in reckless profusion, and the youth often stopped to admire them, and once he picked a handful to take back with him.

"You love flowers," said his father.

"I do, father. Don't you?"

"Somewhat. Your taste comes from your mother. She thought much of them, and when we planted the garden she always planted flower seeds, too." And the trader gave a long sigh as he thought of the good woman who had died so many years before.

Presently they came once more to the burn-over and then made their way straight to the ruins of the old trading-post. The spot looked more forlorn than ever, for the storms of the summer had washed some mud over part of the ground, and grass and weeds flourished amid the blackness.

"That shows what nature can do," observed James Morris. "Give this a few years more and it will be impossible to tell that a post ever stood here. In the same fashion, entire villages have been wiped out, so that historians, going there later, cannot locate even the first sign of the ruins."

An old shovel had been left at the place, and working with this James Morris began to turn over some of the burnt sticks at a spot where he thought he might possibly come upon something of value. In the meantime Dave poked around to suit himself, and presently found two jugs and an iron pot.

"I think these are still good to use," he said, and started down to the creek, to wash them off and inspect them more closely.

He had just reached the creek when a sound in the brushwood beyond caught his ears. He looked up, to see three Frenchmen on horseback riding toward him. The man in advance looked familiar to him, and as this individual drew closer, Dave recognized Jean Bevoir.

CHAPTER XIV

JEAN BEVOIR HAS HIS SAY

Had somebody suddenly arisen from the dead before him, Dave would have been no more astonished than he was when he beheld the Frenchman, who, in the past, had caused him and his relatives so much trouble.

"Jean Bevoir!" he gasped. "But no, it cannot be, for Bevoir was killed at the fall of Montreal!"

The three Frenchmen did not notice the youth until the very edge of the creek was reached. Then Jean Bevoir uttered an exclamation in French.

"Settlers, after all," he said, to his companions.

"Where?" asked both, and came forward, one on each side of him.

By this time Dave was confronting the trio boldly, and now Jean Bevoir looked at him more closely.

"*Parbleu!*" he muttered. "'Tis that Dave Morris, or mayhap I am dreaming!"

"Jean Bevoir!" faltered the youth. "I—I thought you

were dead."

"Dead? And how came you to think that?"

"They told us you were shot down at Montreal."

"Ha! I see. And you were glad of it, not so? But I have disappointed you." The Frenchman paused and then chuckled to himself. "You cannot flee from Jean Bevoir so easily."

"What do you want here?"

"Want, do you ask? What would any honest man want? Yes, I was shot, and left for dead. But my good friends nursed me to health, *malgre moll* And now I am come to claim what is my own."

By this time James Morris had noted the appearance of the newcomers, and leaving his work over the ruins, he walked forward to see who they were.

"Can it be possible that this is Jean Bevoir!" he ejaculated.

"Yes, father," answered Dave. "The report that he was killed was false."

"But the soldiers were so sure—"

"They made a mistake. It is Jean Bevoir beyond any doubt."

"So you are here," declared the Frenchman, glaring darkly at the trader. "I was told that the Englishmen had come no further westward than Fort Duquesne."

"You mean Fort Pitt," answered James Morris pointedly. "Fort Duquesne is a thing of the past." "Some day the fort shall come back to its own," put in one of Bevoir's companions, whose name was Jacques Valette. "You English have but a slim foothold."

"That is a matter of opinion, Valette," answered James Morris. He knew Jacques Valette to be a hunter of the rougher sort, given to much fighting and dissipating. "The war is at an end, and for the present my country is master of the situation."

"The English do not own this land," put in Jean Bevoir. "It has always belonged to the French and the Indians, and it belongs to them still. No army has been sent out here to take possession, and how can the English claim that which they have not even seen or marked out?"

"I won't discuss the old quarrel with you, Bevoir," said James Morris briefly. "We are here to stay, and that is the end of the matter, so far as I am concerned. You can do as you please, but I warn you not to interfere with me. If you do, you will get your fingers burnt."

"The place is burnt down," said the third Frenchman, whose name was Hector Bergerac. He too was a hunter, but of a better sort than Bevoir or Valette. "Shall you build again?"

"Not here," answered James Morris. "I have located a new post on the Ohio."

"The Ohio!" came from the three Frenchmen simultaneously, and the others looked at Jean Bevoir.

"Where upon the Ohio have you placed the new post?" demanded the French trader.

His manner was so insolent that James Morris grew nettled.

"Had you asked me civilly, I would have answered you, Bevoir," he returned. "But now you can find out for yourself."

"We were going to erect a post upon the Ohio," put in Bergerac. "Our pack-train is but a day behind us."

"It will be a loss of time and money for you Frenchmen to do that," came quickly from James Morris. "I tell you that the English are in control, and they mean to keep control. In the end you will lose all you possess."

"We are not for war, but for peace," said Hector Bergerac. "I, for one, will obey the English law, if I find out that that is what must be done."

"*Pouf!*" came from Jean Bevoir. "Show not the heart of a chicken, Bergerac. Remember, we French have still most of the Indians as friends."

"Do you mean to say that you will incite the red men to fight us?" demanded James Morris.

"Ha! that makes you shiver, does it?" cried Jean Bevoir wickedly. "We shall not have to say much, The red men can take their own part. They know well that the French are their true friends, and the English their real enemies."

"You scoundrel!" cried James Morris hotly. "Dare to provoke the red men to fight, and I will see to it that you shall not escape as you did at Montreal. Perhaps you do not know that I have knowledge of your evil doings at Montreal—how you and others tried to loot the stores and private dwellings, and how both the French and the English soldiers turned on you and your dastardly companions and shot you down. How you escaped from justice I do not know, but perhaps, even yet, the authorities will listen to a charge against you."

At this plain outburst Jean Bevoir grew first pale and then crimson. His hand sought the pistol at his side, but the stern look in the English trader's face caused him to drop his hold on the weapon.

"I will not listen to such talk from you!" he exclaimed, grating his teeth savagely. "The story is not true, and you know it. I was wounded while aiding some French people who were sick. I never stole a thing in my life! It is for the English to make up such tales, just to get the French into trouble."

"You wouldn't have to take my word for it," retorted James Morris grimly. "The evidence would rest with those who caught you in the act at Montreal."

"Will you tell us where your post on the Ohio is located?" asked Jacques Valette.

"You heard my answer to Bevoir," returned James Morris. "If you wish to locate, why not do so here? This was a spot Monsieur Bevoir always admired," he added, with some slight show of sarcasm.

"On this burnt-over spot!" ejaculated Jean Bevoir. "No, thank you! I shall go where I expected to go—to the Ohio."

"Rather late in the year to put up a post now," suggested Dave, who could not help saying something.

At this speech Jean Bevoir smiled knowingly.

"Trust me that I know what I am doing," he said. "Come," he added, to his companions, in French. "We can gain nothing by remaining here longer."

He turned his steed around, and rode off, and Valette and Bergerac did the same. Soon the brushwood and forest hid them from view.

"Well, I never!" burst out Dave. "Who would have thought it?"

"It seems we are not clear of that rascal after all," said James Morris bitterly. "Not only is he alive, but he is coming out to his old hunting ground to bother us."

"Do you think he will set up a post near us, father?"

"He did that when I located here. He seems to take savage delight in crowding on my heels."

"That Valette is about as bad a rascal as Bevoir."

"That is true."

"Do you know much of the third fellow?"

"Not a great deal, but I always fancied he was a Frenchman of the better sort. He used to be attached to the fort at Presqu' Isle. I once bought some furs from him, and he was much pleased over what I gave him for them. He said it was much more than Bevoir offered."

"He seems hand-in-glove with Bevoir now."

"Perhaps, or else it may be that he was simply hired by Bevoir to come out and help establish a new post."

"What can they do with winter so close at hand?"

"Nothing much, son. They will have to work hard to provide themselves a shelter."

"Bevoir didn't appear to be much worried."

"He may possibly have something in mind of which I know nothing," answered James Morris thoughtfully. "It is too bad! I wish he would go away and leave me alone. He might just as well establish himself a hundred miles from here, as to be on top of me."

It was now too dark to continue the search around the ruins, and taking the few things they had found with them, they returned to the new post.

"We had better not say anything about Bevoir and his crowd," said James Morris as they journeyed along. "Let the men and the Indians find it out for themselves."

"All right, father; just as you say," answered Dave. "But when they find it out, what then?"

"Then let the men say what they please. We will try to avoid a quarrel."

"Jean Bevoir hates White Buffalo worse than poison."

"I do not doubt it, for White Buffalo accused him several times of cheating the hunters of his tribe out of a reasonable exchange for their furs. Bevoir got the Indians drunk and then literally robbed them."

"He dealt principally in rum, didn't he?"

"Yes; he never gave the Indians anything else if he could help it. All told, I think he was the most rascally trader I ever met in these parts," concluded James Morris.

CHAPTER XV

DAVE'S UNWELCOME VISITOR

For several weeks after that nothing more was seen or heard of Jean Bevoir and his party. More than once James Morris questioned the frontiersmen and Indians in a roundabout manner, asking if they had met any strangers, but the replies were largely in the negative. White Buffalo had once run across a small band of Shawanoes, who had said they would later on come to the post to trade, but that was all.

"Perhaps, after all, Bevoir thought best to move away from this district," said Dave to his parent.

"No, the rascal is not to be gotten rid of so readily," was the answer. "Even if he does not build a post, he will loiter around in the shade until he gets the chance to do me some injury."

There was now a promise of snow in the air, and a few days later the ground was covered to the depth of an inch or more. This made tracking game good, and without delay the frontiersmen and Indians set off to see what they might bring in. As a consequence Dave and Mr. Morris were left at the post alone.

"I am glad the snow held off so long," said James Morris.

"Henry and Barringford must be home by this time—or else close to it."

"If no accidents befell them," said the son.

With the men and Indians away, it was rather lonely around the post for Dave. But there was plenty to do, and the youth kept himself well employed from sunrise to sunset. Occasionally he went fishing in the river with fair success. The log house was made as comfortable as possible, and both worked hard over the stable, that the horses might not suffer when the winter set in in earnest.

Extra timbers had been cut at the top of the hill, back of the trading-post, and when another fall of snow came, James Morris decided to slide these down to where he wanted them.

"If you need me, just call or fire a gun," he said, one morning, and then set off up the hill, taking a team of the strongest horses with him.

After his father was gone Dave took a walk around the post, cleaned some fish he expected to fry for dinner, and looked after the remaining horses. Not a soul appeared to be in sight, and for a little while he felt very lonely indeed. But soon he broke into a cheery whistle, which served to raise his spirits.

"We'll be busy enough as soon as the hunters and trappers begin to bring in their game," he thought. "I hope we do a good business and make some money. Being a soldier didn't pay very handsomely,—and this war has cost father a neat penny."

Returning to the log house from the barn, he was surprised to find the main door wide open. He felt certain that he had closed it on coming away.

"Father, are you there?" he called out, striding forward.

There was no answer, but a second later came a crashing of glass, and looking into the main room of the post he saw Jacques Valette sprawled out on a puncheon bench, with a jug of liquor in his arms and a broken tumbler lying on the floor before him.

"What do you want here?" demanded Dave indignantly.

For the moment Jacques Valette did not answer, but glared at the youth in an uncertain fashion,

"Why do you ask me questions?" he queried in French, and with several hiccoughs.

"Let that liquor alone," went on Dave, now realizing that the French hunter and trapper was more than half intoxicated. "Let it alone, I say!" And he tried to force the jug from Valette's grasp. "Want a drink!" shouted the man, holding tight. "Want a drink! Get me—me some more glass, boy!"

"I will not. Let the jug alone," and now Dave got it in his possession and put it on a high shelf, out of the Frenchman's reach.

With a frightful imprecation in his native tongue Jacques Valette staggered to his feet. He made a clutch for Dave's right ear, but the youth eluded him. Then, in turning, he went sprawling over the puncheon bench, and his head struck the floor, while his feet stuck up in the air.

It was a comical sight, but Dave did not laugh. He realized that he had an ugly customer with whom to deal. He well knew how utterly lawless some of these wild hunters and trappers were when half full of liquor, and knew that they would do almost anything to get more drink with which to finish their debauch. Running to the doorway, he called loudly for his father.

"Stop your noise!" shouted Jacques Valette. "Stop, or I make big trouble!" And he shook his fist at Dave. He was on his feet once more, swaying unsteadily from side to side.

"I want you to go," answered Dave. "Go, do you hear?"

"Give me the jug and I go."

[Illustration: "Let go!" cried Dave. "Let go, I say!"]

"Not a drop. You have had too much already."

"Only haf one glass. Give the jug, like good fellow."

So speaking, Valette lurched over to the shelf and started to bring down the jug once more. But ere he could do so, Dave had him by the arm and was hauling him backward.

In a great rage at being thus thwarted, Jacques Valette began to struggle with the youth. He was a powerful fellow, and for several minutes it looked as if he would get the better of Dave. His hold was a good one, and soon he threw the youth to the floor and held him there.

"Let go!" cried Dave. "Let go, I say!" and did his best to wrench himself free.

It was in the midst of this struggle that James Morris rushed in, having heard Dave's loud cry for assistance. He took in the situation at a glance, and bending down, struck Valette on the side of the head.

"You brute, let my son go!"

Bewildered by the blow, the half-intoxicated Frenchman fell back and Dave staggered to his feet, panting for breath. Valette had caught him by the throat, and the marks of his fingers were still visible.

"What does this mean?" demanded Mr. Morris, after a pause, in which the youth did his best to get back his breath.

In a few words Dave explained. While he was talking, Jacques Valette managed to rise to his feet. If he had been angry before, he was doubly so now. He felt for his pistol, but, luckily, the weapon was gone.

"Ha! you take my pistol," he cried. "Gif it back to me."

"I haven't your pistol," said Dave. "You didn't have one."

"I did. I want it back," growled Jacques Valette.

"You'll get no pistol here," put in James Morris. "You have no right to come to my post and raise a disturbance, and attack my son."

"I want some rum. I pay," returned the Frenchman. "I haf English money—plenty, too!"

With a leer, he put one hand into his outer garment and felt around in a pocket. Then he felt in his other pockets.

"Ha! the money, it is gone!" he cried. "You take my money too! This is the *coup de grace* truly But, *a l'Anglaise!*"

"It is not after the English fashion," put in Dave, who understood the French fairly well. "We are honest people here, and, as my father says, you have no right to come here and raise a quarrel."

"The money—all gone!" muttered Jacques Valette. The loss appeared to sober him for a moment. "Fifteen pounds, ten shillings—all gone!"

"Do you mean to say you had fifteen pounds and ten shillings?" questioned James Morris.

The French hunter and trapper nodded. "*Oui! oui!*"

"And you haven't it now?"

Jacques Valette shrugged his shoulders. "Not a shilling! All is gone! You haf it!" And he shook his hand in Dave's face.

"Don't dare to accuse my son of theft!" exclaimed James Morris angrily. "He has nothing of yours."

A perfect war of words followed. Jacques Valette insisted that, on coming to the post, he had had a pistol and the money mentioned. As they were now gone he felt certain that Dave had taken them. He could not or would not tell where he had been previous to his journey to James Morris' place.

"You lost them before you came here, that is certain," said James Morris. "I want no more from you. Get out!" And he forced the Frenchman to leave. Jacques Valette walked away slowly, muttering all sorts of imprecations in French under his breath.

"He'll try to make us trouble for this," observed Dave, after the unwelcome visitor had gone.

"I have no doubt but that you are right, son." answered

James Morris. "Let us hunt around and see if he dropped his pistol and money anywhere in this vicinity."

A thorough hunt was made, but nothing was found which looked as if it might belong to the Frenchman. Half an hour later it began to snow once more, and soon the tracks made by Jacques Valette were covered up.

"After this I am going to keep the gates barred when we are alone," said James Morris. "I'll hang the horn outside, so anybody who wants to get in can blow." And this was done.

Getting the timbers down the hillside proved no light task, and often Dave went out to aid his father, for they could easily hear the horn at the gate from a great distance. They had also to get in extra firewood for the winter, which promised now to be unusually severe.

It was almost Christmas time before the hunters and trappers who had gone out began to come in with their furs. Among the first to arrive were Lukins and Sanderson, who had managed to bring down a large variety of animals, including two large bears, the pelts of which were worth considerable. These trappers were followed by Jadwin, who had not fared so well, having lost some of his game in the river, and then came White Buffalo and his men, who had been more successful than any of the others. In those days the post became a bustling place, and it really looked as if James Morris' venture would prove a money-making one. He gave fair value for all that was brought to him, and whites and Indians declared themselves well satisfied with their dealings.

Edward Stratemeyer

CHAPTER XVI

DAVE MEETS PONTIAC

It was White Buffalo who brought in the first definite news that the Indians throughout the length and breadth of the Ohio valley, and along the Great Lakes, were becoming dissatisfied with the manner in which the English had taken possession of New France (Canada) and the West.

"White Buffalo has spoken with some of the great chiefs," said he, "and all are agreed that the sky is black for the Indian. With the end of the war the English will push further and further into the forest, and the hunting grounds will be taken away from the red man. The Indian must live by the hunt, so what is he to do?"

"It's the old question over again," answered James Morris. "The Indians won't become farmers, and so they have got to suffer."

"But the Indians claim the land as their own," resumed White Buffalo. "It was left to them by their forefathers. The land of the English lies in England, across the Great Water."

"I hope you don't stand for war, White Buffalo," came from Dave quickly.

"Not for war on the friends of White Buffalo," was the ready answer. "But even White Buffalo cannot stand idly by and see the English take all which belongs to his tribe and to the other red men. The Indian gets nothing in return. He and his squaw and his papoose must live. What should he do? Can my friends tell?"

James Morris gave a sigh. "Honestly, White Buffalo, I cannot. If I could I might solve the whole of this vexing question, and then, perhaps, we'd have no war. But it doesn't seem right for the whites and the Indians to be fighting all the time. It hurts one just as much as it hurts the other."

"My brother James does not tell the truth," said the Indian chief, somewhat sadly. "It hurts the Indian far more than it hurts his white brother. White Buffalo has eyes, and he is wise enough to see that the Indian cannot fight the white man and win in the end. The red man may slay many, but in the end he will lose. I know it, I feel it." And White Buffalo bowed his head.

"Do you look for an uprising soon?" questioned James Morris, after a long pause.

"Not at once—the red men have not forgotten how they suffered during this great war. But it will come—next summer, or the summer after. The red man does not forget that he has suffered."

"Let us hope by next summer the trouble will be forgotten," came from James Morris; and that was all he could say.

Christmas found the post buried deeply in snow, and hunting for the time being was out of the question. The place was crowded, and white trappers and Indians often spent the night in the stable with the horses. There was an

Edward Stratemeyer

active demand upon James Morris' supplies and he could have disposed of three times as many had he had them.

Strange as it may seem, nothing more was heard from Jacques Valette and Jean Bevoir, and the Morrises often wondered what had become of them, and of their companion, Hector Bergerac. They questioned the hunters, both white and red, but could get no information.

"They must have gone up to the Lakes after all," said James Morris. "If it is so, I am thankful for it."

"And so am I thankful," added Dave.

As soon as the weather moderated, the hunters and trappers sallied forth once more, going up and down the Ohio and many miles to the westward. Some of the Indians used their guns as skillfully as the white men, but when powder and ball were scarce they fell back upon their bows and arrows, and it was astonishing what large game they secured.

Once during the winter Dave went out with White Buffalo, on a hunt which lasted three days. They took their bags full of provisions, and the Indian chief led the way across the Ohio and into the depths of the forest, which was entirely new to the youth.

"White Buffalo knows the deer are plentiful here," said the Indian, and so it proved, for before noon they struck the trail of some of the animals, and by nightfall had laid a large buck and his mate low. Then they took up the trail of some other animals and were equally successful.

The evening of the second day's hunt found the pair in the vicinity of an Indian village called Shilagum, standing not far from where the Muskingum River flowed into the Ohio. It was only a small place, but noted among the Shawanoes as the abode of a great medicine man named Paka-Lokalla, or Medicine-of-the-Clouds. The medicine man was an old fellow, with but one ear, and an eye that drooped, but he was looked to as being powerful, and many of the Indians refused to do much without consulting him.

White Buffalo was known in the village, but being of a different tribe he received a cold welcome, until he said he was willing to pay for accommodations for himself and his companion, pointing at the same time to a small skin hanging over his shoulder. At once the Indians bustled about and made the squaws get the visitors something to eat, and made them clean out a small wigwam where the pair might rest for the night.

Dave was suspicious about the wigwam, and especially the old robes offered for bedding, for he had had one unpleasant experience with red men's vermin, as already related in this series. But the wigwam and the robes proved fairly clean after all, and he slept soundly until morning.

When he came forth for his breakfast he was informed by White Buffalo that a most important visitor had arrived at the village. This was none other than Pontiac, the great chief of the Ottawas, who was accompanied by several companions, including Deer Neck, an under-chief of the Wyandots.

Having heard so much about Pontiac, Dave was anxious to see him. He spoke to White Buffalo about the matter and the latter spoke to one of the head men of the village, and a little later both were introduced to the man who, a year and a half later, was to head one of the greatest Indian uprisings known to our history.

At this time Pontiac was between forty-five and fifty years of age, tall, well-formed, and with muscles of iron. His hair

Edward Stratemeyer

was long, his eyes black and penetrating, and his general manner a commanding one. Where he had come from was rather uncertain, although it was generally believed that his father had been either an Ottawa, a Miami, or a Sac, and his mother an Ojibway.

Not only was Pontiac the head of the Ottawas, but he was likewise a chief of the Metais, a powerful organization in the Lake region, the members of which were supposed to be master magicians. To the Metais the ignorant savages humbled themselves as they did to their greatest medicine man.

Of the early history of Pontiac but little can be said. It is doubted if he was a great hunter, although he could use his bow and arrows and a gun with considerable skill. It was as a leader that he shone best. He had uncommon sagacity, good reasoning powers, and a manner of talking that was most persuasive. More than this, his spirit was such that, once having undertaken a project, he would do his best to carry it through, no matter what the cost.

What had brought him to this village Dave did not learn, nor did White Buffalo, for Pontiac said but little so long as they remained at hand. The great chief showed plainly that he wished to be alone with those he had sought out, so White Buffalo and the youth did not prolong their stay longer than was necessary.

As they were about to leave, Pontiac strode forward and glanced sharply at Dave.

"They tell me your father has opened a trading-post on the Ohio." he said in his native tongue.

Dave did not understand, but White Buffalo quickly interpreted the speech.

"He has," answered the youth.

"Does he expect to stay there, or move still further westward?"

"He is going to stay."

At this the great chief gave Dave another close look. Then he turned away and said no more.

"What do you make of this, White Buffalo?" asked Dave, after they had left the Indian village a goodly distance behind them.

"Pontiac likes not the fact that Dave's father has settled down on the Ohio," was the slow answer. "Pontiac wishes the English to keep close to the shores of the Great Waters."

"I must say he looks like a great chief," said the youth thoughtfully.

"He is a great chief, and his power is as wide-spreading as a great summer storm," answered White Buffalo. "The red men everywhere listen to him with all ears."

"Do you suppose he came to see that medicine man?"

"It may be so—he did not tell White Buffalo. But Pontiac is a magician—he can work wonders when he will, so I have heard."

Dave did not believe this, but said nothing on the point to his companion, for he knew it would be useless to attempt to uproot so deep—set a superstition.

"I sincerely hope Pontiac does not try to make trouble for my father," he went on.

"He will do nothing at present—the time is not ripe. The war hatchet is not dug up when the snow covers the ground."

"I know that. But we want no trouble in the spring either."

At this, White Buffalo shrugged his shoulders.

"Who can tell what the moons to come will bring forth?" he said. "The sun comes up and man is alive; it sets, and the last rays fall upon his grave. The Great Spirit of the happy hunting ground rules, but the face of the Great Spirit is hidden from the eyes of the red man and the eyes of the white man as well."

CHAPTER XVII

THE ATTACK ON THE PACK-TRAIN

With the coming of spring, both James Morris and Dave looked eagerly for the time when Henry and Barringford should return to the trading-post with many articles which were much needed, and with what was better yet, news from home.

"I can hardly wait for Henry to get here." said Dave one day. "There is so much I want to know about."

"You must be patient, Dave," returned his parent. "The trails are by no means good yet, and it may be that they have not got started on the journey."

The Indians were now bringing in many beaver skins, to exchange for blankets and powder, but James Morris had nothing to offer them. Many came from a great distance and were much disappointed, so it was not long before the trader looked for the coming pack-train as anxiously as did Dave.

"If they don't come soon, I'll lose what trade I have established," he said. "They will take their skins and furs where they are sure of making an exchange."

Edward Stratemeyer

With the white hunters and trappers it was different. All were willing to trust James Morris, and simply left their goods at the post, to be paid for when the pack-train arrived. It may be added here that Barringford and Henry had been told, in secret, to bring with them one hundred pounds (about five hundred dollars) in gold and silver money, for not a few wanted cash for their pelts.

In the meantime came news that Jean Bevoir and Jacques Valette had been seen among the Indians on the upper Muskingum River. They had done a little trading with the Indians in that neighborhood, and had become very friendly with a young chief named Flat Nose, and with some warriors under him who went by the name of the Wanderers.

"Did you ever hear of this Flat Nose?" asked Dave of the frontiersman who had brought in the information.

"Not I, but Jadwin has," said the hunter. "He says he is as treacherous as they make 'em, and so are all the Wanderers under him. They move from place to place, taking whatever they can lay their hands on."

"Then they will just suit a fellow like Jean Bevoir."

"I don't doubt but that you are right, lad, and they'll suit Jacques Valette, too."

"What has become of Hector Bergerac, do you know?"

"I think he has cut company with Bevoir and Valette. He was too honest for them, I reckon."

In the meantime, matters between the English and the Indians all over the Colonies were going from bad to worse. Those in authority would not listen to such a man as Sir

William Johnson, who knew the red men thoroughly, and such a wise statesman as Benjamin Franklin, who believed in giving the Indian his just due. The war had cost a great deal, and now it was decided to cut down expenses, which meant that in the future the Indians would get but few of the presents which, in the past, had been presented to them. More than this, English traders of all sorts were allowed to go among the red men and barter as they pleased, and some of these literally robbed those who were too ignorant or simple of heart to trade intelligently.

The coming of so many English traders made the French traders furious, and as they saw their business slipping away from them they did all they could to get the English into "hot water" with the red men. They told the Indians that the English meant to take everything from them, their lands, their wigwams, and their possessions, including their squaws and children—to make slaves of the latter—and that the red men must fight or be wiped out. And they always added that, if the Indians would make war, they, the French, would help them in every possible manner.

This was but the empty talk of brutal and ignorant traders, who had everything to gain and nothing to lose. But the Indians listened to them, and at last concluded that it must be so—that the English meant to exterminate them. They held long councils of war, and at last determined to strike a blow at the first favorable opportunity. Pontiac spoke at many of these secret meetings, in a manner that was truly eloquent of the cause he espoused.

"The Indian must fight or he must become as a squaw and a slave," said Pontiac. "The English will press him to the bitter end. They say they are our friends, but they come as wolves in the night to take away our all. You ask how are we to fight them, for they are many? We must use our cunning, we must not let them think we are their enemies. We must

Edward Stratemeyer

treat them as our best friends. Then, when the time is ripe, shall the blow be struck, and no English man, woman, or child shall escape. Pontiac has spoken. Who is there to dispute what he has said?"

The discontent of the Indians was strongest throughout Virginia, Pennsylvania, and New York. The Delawares— those who would not listen to such chiefs as White Buffalo —were angered in the extreme, and the Shawanoes were likewise unsettled. In New York State some simple-minded Indians petitioned Sir William Johnson to have the English forts "kicked out of the way," as they expressed it. This, of course, could not be done, and the red men viewed the strengthening of the strongholds with increased suspicion. Some threats were made to destroy the fort at Detroit, but the time was not ripe for a well-planned attack, and nothing came of it.

At last James Morris could bear the waiting no longer, and leaving Dave and the frontiersman, Sanderson, in charge of the trading-post, he set out with Jadwin on horseback, to see if he could learn anything about the pack-train that was expected.

"Be very careful while I am gone," he said to his son, and Dave promised to do his best.

The route of Mr. Morris and his companion lay through the burn-over, and along the trail previously followed. Good time was made, for their steeds were fresh, and by nightfall they had covered at least twenty-five miles. They went into camp at a convenient spot on the bank of a purling brook, where nothing came to disturb them while they slept. Hardly had they gone two miles in the morning, however, when they came upon a sight that filled them with alarm. Propped up against a tree was Henry, capless, and with the blood streaming over his face from an ugly cut in the forehead.

"Henry! What does this mean?" demanded James Morris.

"Uncle James!" faltered the youth. "Help—help me!"

"To be sure I'll help you, Henry. But what does it mean? Where are Sam and the others, and the horses?"

"We were attacked—some Indians and some white men came upon us at nightfall yesterday. Lampton and Cass, who were with us, were shot down, and Sam was hit and so was I. Our Indians fled into the forest, for the enemy were four to one. Sam and I did what we could, but we had to run. In the darkness we became separated—and here I am."

While Henry was speaking, his uncle was washing his wound, for the youth had stopped near a brook, and now the hurt was bound up with a bit of cloth which was always carried by the trader for just such emergencies. Henry was very weak, and said he had wandered aimlessly about during the night, trying to find the trail to the trading-post. "It may be that Sam is dead," he said sadly. "I know he was struck twice, by a rifle bullet and by an arrow which went into his shoulder. Lampton and Cass, I know, are dead, for I examined them. Conoseka, one of the Indians, was hit in the left arm, but he fled with the other redskins of our party."

"Did you recognize any of those who attacked you?"

"No, for they were in the forest, while we were in a little clearing. The attack came without warning. We were just building a camp-fire when two rifle shots rang out, and Lampton and Cass fell. Then came a yell from the whites and the war cry from the Indians, and shots and arrows flew in all directions. Sam and I picked up our guns, and I know

Edward Stratemeyer

Sam hit one of the whites, for I saw him throw up his hands and fall in some brushwood. Then one of the redskins went down, and after that I was hit and went into a twist, so I can't exactly tell what followed. I heard Sam yell to me to run, or we'd be killed, and I picked up my gun and ran for the trees. I hadn't gone very far when I tripped and fell, and the gun got lost in a dark hollow. I tried to find the gun, but I couldn't, and then I heard some Indians coming after me and I ran on again until I found a small place between the rocks, where I hid until about three hours ago. Then I started to look for the trail, but I got dizzy and had to sit down where you found me."

"You haven't seen any of your party since you ran away?"

"Not a soul. The Indians and Sam ought to be somewhere near, and the pack-train, too, for that matter."

"The rascals must have known the pack-train was coming." said Jadwin, who had been through many fights on the frontier. "To my mind it looks like a well-planned attack."

"That is true," answered James Morris. "The question is, shall we go forward and investigate, or return to the post and give the alarm?"

"Reckon you had better give the alarm. Those rascals may be plannin' to attack the post, too."

"I was thinking of that. But I would like to know what has become of the pack-train and all of my belongings."

"Then, supposing you go ahead alone and take a look around, while Henry and I go to the post?"

This was quickly settled upon, and a few minutes later

James Morris moved onward, on horseback, with his gun ready for use, should the enemy put in an appearance.

Edward Stratemeyer

CHAPTER XVIII

AFTER THE ENCOUNTER

Less than an hour after leaving his nephew and Jadwin, James Morris reached the spot where the fearful encounter of the evening before had occurred.

The spectacle was one to make the heart of any onlooker turn sick, and a shudder passed through the frame of the trader as he gazed at the scene of desolation before him.

Close to the burnt-out camp-fire rested the form of Barnaby Cass, a well-known resident of Winchester, who had followed Barringford to the Ohio district in an endeavor to better his fortunes, A bullet had passed through his heart, and he must have died ere his body struck the ground.

A dozen paces away lay the corpse of the other white man, Oliver Lampton, well known through western Pennsylvania as the Trapper Preacher, because about half of his time was spent in hunting and trapping, and the remainder in preaching temperance to the whites and red men who indulged in liquor to excess. Beside Lampton lay one of the pack-horses, also dead, and another pack-horse lay a little further off, suffering greatly from two broken legs. To put this animal out of its misery James Morris fired a shot into its brain.

Great confusion was on all sides, for many of the packs had been broken open and rifled of their most valuable contents. About half of the stuff had been left behind, principally the goods of the greatest weight. Much that was breakable had been broken, and some valuable blankets that could not be carried off had been slashed and cut with keen knives, in a hasty endeavor to ruin them.

"The rascals!" muttered the trader. "If only we can get on their trail they shall pay dearly for their bloody work here."

Having surveyed the camp, he moved around among the trees and brushwood in the vicinity. He soon found the body of an Indian who had belonged to the pack-train party, and then another Indian who looked to be an enemy. The latter had his face painted in peculiar wavy streaks which the trader had seen twice before.

"The Wanderers!" he muttered. "I half suspected it might be so. This is the work of that rascal Flat Nose—and if that is so, he is moving northward with all speed to get away with his booty. More than likely some French hunters—ha!" He broke off short, for in the undergrowth he had caught sight of another form, that of a white man leaning against a fallen tree, with a gun clutched tightly in his stiffened hands.

"Baptiste Masson!" he muttered, naming a rough French hunter and trapper who, in years gone by, had worked for Jean Bevoir. "As I thought. It was a plot between the Wanderers and the French! They mean to drive me from the Ohio if they possibly can. Masson, eh? Can it be that Jean Bevoir, and Valette, and Bergerac were in it, too? More than likely."

The Frenchman was dead, and James Morris did not hesitate to take his gun and ammunition. He also searched the fellow's pockets, but found nothing of value, nor any clew which might lead to the identity of his companions in the outrage. A further hunt through the forest revealed where something of a struggle had taken place between two white men on foot, but both were gone, and the trail was lost in an adjacent brook, down which one had fled and the other had likely followed, at least for a distance.

The fact that he did not find the body of Sam Barringford gave James Morris hope. If the old frontiersman was not seriously wounded it was more than likely he was on the trail of those who had attacked the pack-train, with a view to finding out where they were going, or to ascertain exactly who was responsible for the affair.

"I know Sam will do what he can," he thought, and with this small degree of comfort he loaded his steed with such things as he could carry and started on the return to the trading-post.

It was a hard journey, and he did not reach the Ohio until long after nightfall. He found the post being guarded by five frontiersmen and eight Indians, who had been hastily called together as soon as Henry and Jadwin appeared.

"Father!" cried Dave joyfully, as he ran to meet his parent. "I am glad you are back safe."

"Has Henry come?"

"Yes, and I made him lie down, he was so weak. What an awful fight it must have been! Did you discover who did it?"

"Partly. One of the dead redskins was a Wanderer, and a dead white man was that good-for-nothing Baptiste Masson I have often mentioned to you."

"The fellow who traveled with Jean Bevoir?"

"The same. I am inclined to think that the attack was organized by Flat Nose, of the Wanderers, and Bevoir. If you'll remember, Jadwin said Flat Nose, Bevoir, and Valette were very friendly."

"What about Sam?"

"I couldn't find any trace of him, although I looked around pretty well."

"Sam carried fifty pounds of the money you sent for. Henry has the rest of it safe."

"I am glad of that. But I wish I knew about Sam. He may have run himself into a regular hornet's nest."

Nothing had happened to disturb those at the post itself, and James Morris lost no time in sending out two white men and two Indians, with horses to bring in what was left on the trail of his belongings.

It was found that Henry was not seriously wounded, and after a good night's sleep the youth felt much better. His mind was now clearer, and he related all the particulars of the attack as far as he knew them.

"I should judge there must have been, at least, six white men and twenty Indians," he said.

"They ran from tree to tree and had us at a disadvantage from the very start. I should have been shot dead if I hadn't got behind one of the horses. The redskins set up a fearful din after the white men shot off their guns. I was afraid every one of us would be killed and scalped."

"Thank God that you escaped!" murmured James Morris, and Dave breathed a silent amen. The following day found

James Morris more impatient than ever to learn what had become of Sam Barringford. He wanted to go on a search for the old frontiersman, yet he did not deem it advisable to leave the trading-post, fearing that an attack might come during his absence.

"I will go out for you," said Jadwin "I'd do 'most anything fer Sam Barringford. We have hunted and fit Injuns fer twenty-five years and more."

"And I'll go with Tony," put in Ira Sanderson. "I think we can hit the trail if any white men can."

The matter was talked over for fully an hour, and Dave took in what was said with deep interest.

"Father, let them go, and let me go with them," he said. "You know what I think of Sam. If he is in trouble, I want to aid him if it can possibly be done."

"You'll be safer here, Dave."

"Perhaps, but let me go, won't you?"

Dave continued to plead, and in the end it was settled that he should accompany Tony Jadwin and Ira Sanderson on the scouting tour. The three were to go on horseback, and were to return inside of four or five days, unless a turn of circumstances made it necessary to stay away longer.

"You take good care of yourself, Dave," said Henry, who was sitting on a bench with his head bound up. "Those Indians are on the warpath, and they mean business."

"Well, I'll mean business too, if I get a chance at them," replied the youth, with a short laugh.

From Henry it was learned that all at the Morris homestead were well. The twins were now able to walk and were very cute. In spite of all that had been done to learn something of their parentage, the mystery surrounding their identity was as thick as ever. A few inquiries had been made concerning them, but nobody had come forward to claim the pair.

"I reckon they are going to be Sam's twins after all," said Henry. "That is, unless something has happened to Sam. If he's dead—but no, I can't think that, can you?"

"I cannot," answered Dave soberly. "He's our best chum, isn't he? Oh, he must be alive!" He paused a moment. "But if he isn't, I reckon we'll have to keep the twins for him."

"Of course we'll have to keep the twins. My, but they are funny little chaps! Nell thinks the world of them, and mother and Rodney are just about as bad. I think, behind it all, the folks would rather keep them than have somebody come and take them away," concluded Henry.

Preparations for the departure were soon complete, and the party left the trading-post in the morning, long before the sun was up. It had been decided that they should go straight to the spot where the attack had taken place, and from that point do their best to learn what had become of Sam Barringford, and of the men who had run away with the goods.

"Remember, my son, to keep out of danger if you can possibly do so," was James Morris' final warning. "I would rather lose my goods a dozen times over than have anything serious happen to you."

"I'll do my best," answered Dave; and a moment later he rode away, little dreaming of the surprises in store for him.

Edward Stratemeyer

CHAPTER XIX

THE TRAIL THROUGH THE FOREST

It can truthfully be said that at the time of which I write, no hunter on the trail was more keen-eyed among the whites than Antonio Jadwin, who had been chosen as leader of the little expedition.

Tony Jadwin, as he was familiarly called, was English by birth, but had come to America while but a child of four. His folks had settled on the frontier, and both had been massacred in an uprising when the lad was less than sixteen. Tony had at once started in as a hunter and trapper on his own responsibility, and from that day to the present time had managed to earn for himself a comfortable if not a luxurious living.

He took to all sorts of shooting, trapping, and fishing as the proverbial duck takes to water, and could follow a deer trail almost in the dark. He had brought down all sorts of game, and his left shoulder showed deep scars dating back to a fierce face-to-face fight with a bear, in which he had, after a tough struggle, come off victorious.

Having arrived at the scene of the attack, Jadwin took a close survey of the situation, going over the ground far more observantly than had James Morris. Nothing escaped his keen eyes, and he quickly announced that Henry had probably been right in his estimate of the number of the enemy. He also pointed out Barringford's footsteps, and declared that the old frontiersman had most likely followed the others, after the pack-train was overhauled and looted.

It was nightfall by the time all these observations were made, and the three decided to go into camp at a convenient spot, not far away. While Dave prepared supper the others dug a large grave, and into this the bodies of Cass and Lampton were placed, and a stone was set up to mark the spot.

Jadwin would not allow all to sleep at once, declaring that a watch was necessary. "I'll stay awake a few hours, and then call Ira," said he, "and then Ira can call Dave." And so it was arranged.

Dave was tired by the hard journey, and it was not long before he was sound asleep. He did not awaken until four in the morning, when Sanderson aroused him.

"Why didn't you call me before?" he cried, leaping up. "I want to do my full share of duty while I am out with you."

"It's all right, lad," answered the other. "I'm not very sleepy myself, but a couple of hours won't do me any harm."

A brook was close by, and at this Dave took a washing up, which made him wide-awake. Then he began to gather some sticks with which to start up a blaze in order to cook the morning meal.

He had taken up half a dozen sticks when a sound not very far away caught his ears. He was on the alert instantly, thinking it might perhaps be some wild animal. A dozen paces away was his gun, and he dropped the firewood and caught up the weapon.

Hardly had he done so, when he saw the form of a burly French hunter stealing through the forest toward the spot where the attack had been made on the pack-train. Fortunately, the Frenchman did not look toward Dave, so he and his companions, and their steeds, were not discovered.

"That fellow is up to no good, that is certain," thought the youth, and lost no time in arousing his companions.

"A Frenchman, eh?" said Jadwin. "More'n likely one of the crowd come back to see if he can't take away what was left of the loot."

Making no noise, they followed the Frenchman, who was dressed in the conventional garb of the hunters of the Great Lakes. The newcomer moved forward swiftly, and they had all they could do to keep up with him.

The spot reached, the Frenchman gazed around with evident dismay. Probably he had expected to see what had been left of the pack-train still there.

"Gone!" he muttered, in his native tongue. "I have had my trip of thirty miles for nothing."

After a careful look around, he returned to the forest, and set off at a quick pace in the direction from whence he had come.

"Shall we leap upon him and make him a prisoner?" asked Dave, in a whisper.

"No," replied Jadwin shortly. "Keep quiet."

Dave now understood what was in the trapper's mind, and kept still, and in a moment more the Frenchman was out of sight, moving swiftly to the northwest.

"I will follow him on foot and blaze the trail with my hunting knife," said Jadwin, to Dave and Sanderson. "You can come after me with the horses. He will probably go straight to where the rest of the rascals are in camp."

In a minute Jadwin was off and the others were not slow to follow. As before mentioned, the trail led to the northwest, through an unusually thick growth of sycamores and hemlocks. Fortunately the way was well defined, being used by many wild beasts, in their trips between the Ohio and the Great Lakes.

The French hunter and trapper was a rapid walker, and Tadwin did not catch sight of the fellow for two hours after starting on the trail. Then he located the man sitting on a slight knoll, resting. He at once halted and kept his position until the Frenchman moved again, when he followed as before.

During the entire day the following was kept up in this fashion. Late in the afternoon the Frenchman stopped to prepare himself a meal, building a tiny fire between some stones for that purpose. Seeing this, Jadwin walked back a short distance and there met Dave and Sanderson, who had followed his blazed trail without difficulty.

"He's a good walker," was Dave's comment, as the three partook of food themselves. "How much further do you think he'll go to-night?"

At this query Jadwin shrugged his shoulders. "Tell you that, Dave, after he goes to sleep," he answered dryly.

The horses were tethered, and all three stole forward to take another look at the stranger. To their surprise he had sunk back in some bushes beside his little fire and was fast asleep.

"He is not going very much further to-night," whispered Dave. "Just listen to him snore!"

A consultation was held, and Dave was for stealing up while the man slept and seeing if his pockets contained anything which might lead to his identity. Jadwin and Sanderson were willing, and watched the young pioneer with deep interest as he moved slowly forward, screening himself by the very bushes that served the sleeping man as bed and pillow.

The Frenchman slept soundly, so the youth ran but a small risk of awakening him. With great caution he searched one pocket after another, finding a small amount of silver and several letters. With these he returned to Jadwin and Sanderson, and the three withdrew to look over the communications.

Tony Jadwin could read a little French, and in his labored manner he spelt out the two letters Dave had captured. By these they learned that the Frenchman was named Louis Glotte and that he belonged at Detroit, the settlement taken from the French by the English after the fall of Montreal. Both spoke of money to be made out of the English and were signed "Jean."

"That must mean Jean Bevoir!" cried Dave. "This Glotte must be another of Bevoir's rascally companions."

"To be sure," put in Sanderson, "And Bevoir must mean the attack that was made on the pack-train."

"I think he will rejoin Bevoir by to-morrow sure," said Tony

Jadwin. "And then we may learn what has become of Sam."

While one or another remained on guard during the night the others slept. Dave, it must be admitted, was impatient to learn what had really become of his old frontier friend, and it was some time before he could bring himself to slumber. Near at hand was an owl hooting weirdly through the night. Under ordinary circumstances they would have scared the bird away, but now they did not dare, for fear of arousing Louis Glotte's suspicions.

The sun was just coming up when Sanderson called softly to the others. "He's moving," said the hunter, and in a few minutes Jadwin took to the trail as before, and the others came after with the horses.

The way was now more difficult than ever, and they had numerous small streams to cross. Then they came to a river, and before Jadwin could catch sight of the Frenchman again the fellow was in a canoe and hurrying to the other side.

"Now we are in a pickle truly," declared Dave. "How are we to get to the other side without a boat?"

"Wait until he's out of sight and I will show you," answered Jadwin.

Louis Glotte soon disappeared among the bushes, and then Jadwin led the way to where a fallen tree lay. "Tie up the horses," he ordered, and it was done. Next the tree trunk was pushed into the stream and all straddled it. By means of rude paddles cut from tree boughs they ferried themselves to the opposite shore.

"Wait! I see something!" murmured Dave, after having gone through the bushes which lined the water's edge.

"So I do see something," came from Jadwin. "Lay low until I investigate, boys."

Dave and Sanderson secreted themselves in the bushes and waited. Tony Jadwin disappeared and it was the best part of half an hour before he returned.

"Just as I thought," he said. "The Frenchmen and the Indians have a village back there, on the bank of a creek that flows into this river. Jean Bevoir is there, and also Jacques Valette, and I rather think all the stolen goods are there also."

CHAPTER XX

GUARDING THE TRADING-POST

"Did you see anything of Sam Barringford?" asked Dave, who was just then thinking more of his old friend than of his father's belongings.

"I did not. But I shouldn't be surprised if those Frenchmen and redskins had some prisoners," answered Jadwin. "They have one wigwam that they are guarding closely. If it doesn't contain prisoners, it contains something of great value."

For quarter of an hour the frontiersmen and Dave talked over the situation, but could not solve the problem of what was best to do next.

"To attack would be foolhardy, even if we hid ourselves among the trees," said Sanderson. "They'd drive us from cover sooner or later, and kill us."

"One of us might go back for help," suggested the young pioneer.

"I was thinking of that. But that would take time, and your father couldn't spare enough men to make it worth while. As near as I can make out there are six Frenchmen in the camp and nineteen red men, or twenty-five fighters in all.

The most we could muster up would be ten or a dozen. That would be two to one."

"If they have any captives, and especially Sam Barringford, I wish we could release them."

"Let us wait until nightfall," suggested Ira Sanderson. "Something may turn up."

Not far away was a slight rise of ground, and behind some bushes on this they hid themselves. From this quarter they could get a fair view of the village and note much of what was going on.

They had scarcely settled themselves when they heard a shout, and an Indian who had been on guard came in with another Indian, who had just arrived on foot from a distance.

"It is an Ottawa!" murmured Jadwin. "One of the braves of Pontiac's tribe."

"He evidently has news," said Dave. "I wish we knew what it was."

Jadwin decided to crawl to another spot and learn if he could overhear what was being said.

This time he was gone the best part of an hour, nor did he return until Dave and Sanderson saw the strange Indian messenger depart.

"What did you learn?" asked the youth eagerly.

"A great deal," answered Jadwin hurriedly.

"We must get back to the trading-post without delay."

"Why?"

"The Indians are going to make an attack. The Miamis are up in arms. Pontiac has told them that if they do not destroy the forts and trading-posts the English will soon wipe them from the face of the earth."

"The Old Nick take Pontiac!" ejaculated Sanderson.

"I'd like to get on his trail and make him a prisoner," put in Dave.

"Another thing, Sam Barringford is Bevoir's prisoner."

"Are you certain?"

"Yes. I heard Bevoir speak of it to another Frenchman. He says he will make Barringford suffer before he is done with him."

"Oh, the rascal!" burst out Dave. "I wish—"

"Never mind, lad, I know how you feel. But every moment is precious. We must hasten to the post and prepare for the attack."

"Yes! yes! Come!" and Dave himself led the way.

Not to excite the suspicions of either red men or white, they did not use the canoe which was at hand, but recrossed the stream on the tree trunk which had brought them over in the first place. This done, they cast the tree adrift and lost not a moment in mounting their steeds.

"'Tis a long, long ride," said Jadwin. "But if the horses can make it without a night's rest, so much the better for us and for all of the others."

It proved a ride that Dave Morris never forgot. All that day and through the night the three pressed on, through the mighty forests and across the creeks and small rivers. More than once a horse would stumble and almost throw his rider, and the branches of the trees often cut them stinging blows across the faces and necks and hands. Once Dave received a long scratch on the left cheek from which the blood flowed freely, but he did not stop to bind up the wound, nor did he complain.

"To save father, and Henry, and the post!" Such was the burden of his thought. He remembered how that other post, on the Kinotah, had been attacked. Should the new post fall, he well knew that it would go hard with all who had stood to defend it.

When at last the post was gained Dave was more dead than alive. Chafed by his hard ride, and almost exhausted, he tumbled rather than leaped from the saddle. It was the middle of the night and the coming of the three had provoked a small alarm, so that all at the trading-post came to learn what was in the air.

Jadwin's story was soon told, and Dave and Sanderson corroborated it. Without delay James Morris called the whites and Indians around him.

"There is news that the French and Indians intend to attack this post," he said loudly. "Will you help me to save what is my own, or must I surrender?"

At once there was a hubbub. White Buffalo was the first to step to the trader's side.

"White Buffalo will fight for his brother James," said the Indian chief simply. "And his braves will fight also," and he motioned for the other Indians to follow him.

"I'm for the post, every time," cried Jadwin. "If I hadn't been, I shouldn't have been in sech a hurry to get back."

"Ditto myself," put in Sanderson.

"I reckon we air all with you," drawled one of the trappers. "We want an English tradin'-post hyer, eh, boys?"

"That's the tune," added another. "The only question is, air we strong enough for 'em?"

"Got to be!" exclaimed Sanderson emphatically. "I'll fight 'em for all I know how!" muttered Henry. His rest had done him much good.

The details of the defense were quickly arranged, for James Morris had often speculated upon just what to do in such a situation as was now at hand. Everything left outside of the palisade was brought in and then the gates were closed, barred, and reenforced by large rocks which lay handy. This accomplished, every gun and pistol in the post was examined, cleaned, and put into perfect order for use, and powder and ball were dealt out liberally. The Indians also looked after their bows and arrows, and hunting knives and tomahawks were not forgotten.

By the time arrangements were all complete, the sun was shining in the eastern sky. Hour after hour passed and no strangers put in an appearance.

"But they will come, never fear," said Jadwin. "I've made no mistake."

"Somebody coming now!" shouted James Morris, who was near the gate. A moment later an Indian came strolling along the bank of the river. Evidently he had expected to find the gate to the stockade wide open. Seeing it closed, he hesitated for a moment.

"*Hoola! hoola!*" he shouted. "Brown Bear come to trade!"

"Where are your furs?" asked James Morris, mounting some steps so that he could see over the gate.

"Furs in canoe on river," answered Brown Bear. His eyes were full of distrust and suspicion.

"You are one of the Wanderers, I believe," said James Morris. "You trade with the French, not with the English."

"Trade with English now," said the red man doggedly.

"You can't trade here, so pass on."

"No take furs from Brown Bear?"

"No."

"Make much cheap trade. Buffalo skin, too, an' bear."

"Bring them up till I see them."

"White man open gate."

"Show me your buffalo and bear skins," was all James Morris would answer.

With a grunt of disgust Brown Bear walked away and disappeared among the bushes.

"Do you think he really has the furs?" asked Henry. "I don't."

"No, Henry. He came to report what we were doing. He is a

spy. We'll see some more of them soon."

Mr. Morris was right; half an hour later another Indian, accompanied by Louis Glotte, came into view from over the hill.

"Open the gate! Want to trade!" cried the Indian.

"Vat for you close ze gate, Meester Morris?" asked Glotte smoothly. "No fighting now, no!" And he laughed shortly.

"No, I don't reckon there will be any fighting," answered the trader. "But if it comes, I am ready for it. The Indian can't come in, but you can, if you wish." And he threw a ladder over the gate, keeping hold of the top.

Not knowing what a trap he was walking into, Louis Glotte spoke to the Indian in his native tongue and then mounted the ladder. As soon as the Frenchman was inside of the stockade James Morris returned the ladder to its original position.

"Don't you come too near!" he shouted to the Indian, and waved him away.

"I'll keep an eye on him, never fear," said Sanderson, who was at one of the port-holes.

"What want you of me?" demanded Glotte, as he gazed around at the armed English and Indians in dismay.

"I want to talk to you," replied James Morris. "Come into the cabin with me."

More suspicious than ever, the Frenchman followed into the building slowly. Dave came after and so did Jadwin.

"Now, Glotte, you can consider yourself a prisoner," said James Morris shortly. "Place your gun on that table, and your pistol also."

CHAPTER XXI

SAM BARRINGFORD BRINGS NEWS

Louis Glotte understood the true situation at last, and the cold sweat stood out on his forehead. James Morris had a pistol in his hand, and the Frenchman saw that all of the others were also armed.

"So I am your prisonair?" he said slowly. "For vat, tell me zat?"

"You know well enough," put in Dave.

As James Morris' pistol came up the Frenchman's gun was placed on the rough table and his pistol followed. Glotte might have showed fight, but he saw that such a course would be worse than useless. He had walked into a neat trap and with his eyes wide open.

"Louis Glotte," said James Morris sternly, "I want you to tell me the truth, do you hear? If you do not tell me the plain truth, you shall suffer."

"Vat ees it you vant?"

"Who organized the attack on my pack-train?"

"I know nothing of zat."

"Stop! You do know, and you must tell me."

The Frenchman grew pale and something like a shiver passed over him. He saw that James Morris was in no mood for trifling.

"Who—who say zat Louis Glotte know 'bout dat?" he asked stammeringly.

"I say so. You were there, for one."

"No! no! I—I vas far away!"

"Tell me who organized the attack."

"I—I cannot!"

"You can."

"No! no! I—I—I—Stop! Do not shoot me! I vill tell! Eet vas Jean Bevoir."

"I thought as much. Was Jacques Valette with him?"

"*Oui!* But say not I tell you, or za vill keel me!"

"And Hector Bergerac?"

The Frenchman shook his head. "Not Bergerac, no. He ees gone avay."

"Who were the others?"

After Considerable hesitation Louis Glotte named them over. Then James Morris questioned him concerning the

Wanderers and learned that they had been headed by their chief, Flat Nose. The other red men he knew little about, but he said they were a dirty, irresponsible tribe, willing to do almost anything for the sake of getting provisions or rum.

"They think ze pack-train carry much rum," said Glotte. "Verra mad when za found out not so."

In the end he told practically all he knew, being assured that he would not be harmed if he made a full confession. Jean Bevoir and Flat Nose had led the attack, in which four of their party had been killed or wounded. What had been taken away was removed under the directions of Bevoir and taken to an Indian village "many miles away," as he expressed it. He said the red men were about a hundred and fifty strong, and had made Sam Barringford a prisoner. Of course he knew nothing of the visit of Dave, Jadwin, and Sanderson to the place, nor did James Morris enlighten him.

The trader then insisted upon knowing if an attack upon the trading-post was contemplated, and Glotte at last confessed that such was a fact. The man was a thorough coward at heart and willing to do almost anything in order to save his own life.

"We shall have to make you a prisoner for the present," said James Morris, and without ceremony Glotte's hands were bound behind him and he was tied to a strong post used for hitching purposes.

The Indian who had come up with the Frenchman had retreated to the forest, and for the time being not a human form was to be seen anywhere outside of the palisade. But the English did not relax their vigilance.

"Perhaps they'll wait until night to begin the attack," said

Edward Stratemeyer

Henry. "The redskins love to fight under cover of darkness—we know that too well."

"Or else the report that the gate is closed and the place guarded will dishearten them," returned his cousin.

Hour after hour went by and night came on. A stricter watch than ever was kept, but as before neither Indian or Frenchman showed himself. More than this, the night birds and owls uttered their cries as usual, mingled with the bark of a fox and the mournful howling of several wolves, all of which told that the vicinity was most likely entirely free from human beings.

"They wanted to catch us unawares, and they have discovered their mistake," said one frontiersman; and such was probably the case, for the whole of the night and the following morning passed without further alarm.

Some of those at the post were now impatient to go out and follow up the enemy, but others demurred, stating that their numbers were too small.

"If those wretches are in hiding, they'd wipe us out in no time," said Sanderson. "Better stay where we are for the present."

Nevertheless James Morris and Tony Jadwin went out, on a short scouting expedition, along the river and then for a few hundred feet into the forest. They advanced with great caution, taking care not to expose themselves in the open, and carrying their guns ready for use, should any of the enemy show themselves.

"We cannot afford to take many chances," said James Morris, as they moved forward. "Our force at the post is too small."

"Wish we had a company of Royal Americans here, to knock 'em out," said Jadwin.

Three hours were spent on the scouting tour, and both of the men were on the point of turning back to the fort, satisfied that the Frenchmen and Indians had indeed given up the proposed attack, when they heard the sound of rapid footsteps, and a man burst into view, running with all his might and main.

"Halt!" cried James Morris, who at the first sound had raised his musket, while Jadwin did the same.

"Don't shoot!" came back, in the well-known voice of Sam Barringford.

"Sam!" cried the trader, lowering his weapon, "what does this mean?"

"It means I'm 'most out o' breath with runnin'" gasped the old frontiersman. "But git to the post—the French and Indians air a-comin'!"

Sam Barringford had come up close to the others, and now without more words all three headed for the post. It was easy to discern that the old frontiersman was well-nigh exhausted, and he was glad enough to take hold of James Morris' shoulder on one side and Tony Jadwin's on the other.

"Been a prisoner of them skunks, fire burn 'em!" he explained. "I'll tell ye all about it later. Have ye heard o' Henry, an' the others?"

"Yes, Henry is safe and so are most of the others. Cass and Lampton are dead. We were afraid you had been killed, too, until Louis Glotte told us you were a prisoner." And then

James Morris told of the manner in which Dave, Jadwin, and Sanderson had followed up the trail.

"Glad ye got Glotte a prisoner," said Barringford. "He is 'most as mean a skunk as Jean Bevoir."

They now came in view of the post and were quickly admitted by those on guard.

"Sam Barringford!" cried Dave and Henry in a breath, and ran up to greet their old friend.

After he had been fed and allowed to rest a bit, Barringford told his story in detail. He said he had followed Jean Bevoir and the others to the river near which the Indian village was located. A stray Indian dog had exposed his hiding place, and after a desperate fight in which one Indian had been killed and he himself had been cut in the shoulder with a tomahawk, they had succeeded in making him a prisoner. He had been put into the wigwam already mentioned, with his hands bound behind him and to a stake driven deeply into the soil. He knew of the message sent in by Pontiac, and added that numerous other attacks were to be made on forts and settlements throughout the West.

"But how did you get away?" asked Dave.

"Easier nor I expected," was the old frontiersman's answer. "As soon as it was settled the post should be attacked there was some confusion, and the guard left the wigwam. I yanked and pulled with all my might and at last the stake came out of the ground. Then I rolled to the back of the wigwam and slipped under the skins to some bushes. As soon as I was that far, I got on my feet and legged it for all I knew how. I ran along the river for about a mile, because I didn't know how to get across with my hands tied. At last I got the rawhides loose and slipped 'em, and then I came over at a shallow spot where I didn't have to swim but a few yards. I ran as fast as I could, for I didn't know how soon the attack would start."

"Something has gone wrong, or they would be here by this time," put in Sanderson.

Glotte viewed the coming of Sam Barringford with great astonishment. "How you geet avay?" he asked.

"That is my business, Glotte," answered the old frontiersman. "I reckon you thought I couldn't do it, eh?" And he chuckled to himself.

"Zat fellow ees a sharp one," was the Frenchman's comment. "He ees like ze flea to slip avay, *oui!*"

Throughout the remainder of the night the guard remained as watchful as ever. But it was labor lost, for neither French nor Indians showed themselves.

At daybreak White Buffalo said he would go out on another scouting tour, taking with him two of his braves. They moved off by the way of the river bank and then made a large semicircle, returning to the post from a diametrically opposite direction.

"Wanderers and bad Frenchmen all gone," announced the chief, on coming back. "They came, but did not fight."

"Do you mean to say that they have been here?" cried James Morris.

White Buffalo nodded several times. "Five canoes come down the river, land by the four big trees. The trail is in the mud and the wet grass—so many Frenchmen"—he held up five fingers—"and so many Indians"—holding up both hands twice and then four fingers, a total of twenty-four.

"Where did they go to?" asked Henry.

"Go into the woods and stand. Two walk around to the hill—one canoe land on other side of river and Indians go up past the post—then come back. Then all gone once more. Afraid to fight! The Frenchmen and the Wanderers are cowards!" And the face of the Delaware showed his deep disdain.

"It must be true," put in Sanderson. "They most likely met the Indian who came here first, and then the fellow with Glotte, and both told 'em it would be of no use—that we were too strong for them."

"Well, if they are gone, I hope they don't come back again," said Dave, and a number standing around echoed the sentiment.

CHAPTER XXII

THE ROCK BY THE RIVER

The Indians did not return, and in forty-eight hours the scare was over, and the hunters and trappers sallied forth from the trading-post as before, confident that Sanderson had been right,—that the enemy had thought the little garrison too strong for them.

But this was a mistake. Jean Bevoir and Flat Nose had been eager for the fight, but word had come in at the last moment that the attack must be put off, and such was the power of Pontiac and other great chiefs of that vicinity that Flat Nose obeyed. As it was impossible for the handful of Frenchmen under Bevoir to do anything alone the whole scheme fell through, and then Bevoir lost no time in getting back to where he had left the loot from the pack-train, claiming that which had been allotted to him and his men, and getting away further to the northwestward, where he felt tolerably safe from pursuit.

How far the conspiracy to fall upon the English on the frontier in the summer of 1762 was concocted by Pontiac will perhaps never be known. Some historians have contended that he was responsible for it in its entirety, while others have told us that the real Pontiac conspiracy was confined to the awful uprising which took place just one

Edward Stratemeyer

year later. But be that as it may, it is undoubtedly true that Pontiac hated the English intensely and that it galled him exceedingly to see them pushing further and further to the north and the west. His own lands around the Great Lakes were being invaded, and when his tribe went to the English for redress they got but scant attention.

The summer of 1762 proved to be one of anxiety and uncertainty for all on or near the frontier. To the northward the Iroquois, or Mingoes as they were commonly called, were held in check by Sir William Johnson, but in western New York and western Pennsylvania the Wyandots, the Shawanoes, and certain tribes of the Delawares did what they could to harass the pioneers, burning cabins and sheds at night, stealing crops and cattle, and occasionally murdering men, women, and children, or carrying the latter off into captivity. There were no battles, but the pioneers and frontiersmen retaliated, and as winter came on the feeling of bitterness increased. No one felt safe, and all wondered what new outrage would happen next.

The Delawares have been mentioned as taking part in these evil doings, and as White Buffalo and his followers were Delawares, it is but right that their standing should be explained. In years gone by the Delawares had been a mighty tribe, numbering over a hundred villages of importance. But internal strife had done its work, and now the villages were widely scattered, so that Delawares could be found from Virginia in the South to the Great Lakes in the North and as far west as the Mississippi. Those who remained near the eastern coast generally sided with the English, while the others either strove to remain neutral or threw in their fortunes with the French.

It must not be supposed that James Morris allowed matters to rest after it became known that no attack would be made upon the trading-post. He wished to recover the stolen goods and also the fifty pounds which had been taken from Sam Barringford by Jean Bevoir at the time the old frontiersman was a prisoner at the Wanderers' village.

An expedition was organized, consisting of the trader and seven whites and Indians, and they remained out the best part of a week, hunting for the Wanderers and for Bevoir and his companions. But the Wanderers had moved and Bevoir had likewise disappeared, and the trail was lost at the river bank.

"I suppose I can say good-by to both money and goods," said James Morris soberly. "I declare, it's too bad!"

"I'll try to make it right with ye about the money," said Barringford.

"No, Sam, I don't want you to do that. You did your best and it's not your fault that the money is gone, nor the goods either. But I'd give a few pounds to get hold of Bevoir and his crowd."

As the days went by it was decided by James Morris not to send to the East for more goods until late in the fall, the goods to be brought to the trading-post early in the spring. Louis Glotte was allowed his liberty and immediately disappeared.

Both Dave and Henry were very anxious to go out on a regular hunt with Barringford, and this was arranged for several weeks after it became positively known that all hostile whites and red men had left the neighborhood of the trading-post. The hunting tour was to last a week or ten days, and the young pioneers made their preparations accordingly.

"Sam, we must get a buffalo this trip," said Henry.

"Nothing less will satisfy me."

"Easier said nor done, lad," answered the old frontiersman. "The hunters an' trappers have scart 'em putty far to the westward. Howsome-ever, we can try our best to lay one low."

"I want to get a bear," said Dave.

All were feeling in fine spirits when the start was made, and James Morris came out of the post to see them off. All were on horseback, for Barringford had said that a buffalo hunt was generally in the open where riding was fairly good.

"Now don't you get into any more trouble," were Mr. Morris' parting words. "We've had trouble enough to last us a lifetime."

"We'll do our best to steer clear of it," answered his son.

The evening of the first day found them in a territory that was entirely new to both Dave and Henry, although Barringford had been over the ground several times. Only some small game had been seen, not worth powder and shot, as the old frontiersman put it, and they made their evening meal from some fish which Henry managed to catch. While Barringford was preparing the fish, both of the young pioneers took a swim in the river, where the water was cool and refreshing.

"This is something like!" cried Dave, as he splashed around.

"You're right there," answered Henry. "Only I don't want any more wildcats tumbling down on my head from the trees," he continued, referring to an adventure which has already been told in "Marching on Niagara."

"I don't believe there are any wildcats around here, Henry. The place seems utterly deserted. I reckon we'll have to travel a day longer before we strike game. The old hunters have been over the ground too thoroughly."

"It's not half as bad as it will be, when more settlers come here."

"That is true."

The young pioneers felt in fine spirits, and as Barringford was slow in getting the evening meal prepared, Henry proposed a swimming match.

"I'll race you to yonder big rock and back!" he cried, pointing to a round stone resting on the opposite bank, under a thick, overhanging tree. "The best piece of fish in the pan to the one who wins!"

"Done!" returned Dave. "Are you ready to start?"

"Yes. But wait, let us call Sam, and he can start us." And he yelled to the old frontiersman.

"Want to race, eh?" said Barringford. "All right, if ye ain't too tired after sech a ride as we've had. All ready? Then go it, both on ye! Go!"

Away they went, side by side, each cutting the clear water with a firm, broad stroke, for both could swim well.

"It's goin' to be nip an' tuck, I reckon!" went on Barringford, as interested as if the youths were matched for a heavy purse. "I must say I don't know who to shout for! Do your best, both on ye! Now, Dave, that won't do!"

For Dave had fallen behind a few strokes. But Henry could

Edward Stratemeyer

not keep the speed at which he had started, and slowly but surely his cousin reached his side once more and then went a foot and more ahead.

"Henry, this won't do!" sang out the old frontiersman. "Don't you let Dave git the best on ye! Strike out an' make it a tie!"

Thus encouraged, and laughing to himself, Henry put on another spurt, and while Dave was still four yards from the big rock came up alongside as before.

"Now ye have it!" roared Barringford. "Keep the pace, both on ye! The feller to lose gits walloped, an' the winner gits the King's Cross an' a purse of a thousand pounds! Tech the rock fair an' squar', or I'll call the race off!" And Barringford slapped his thigh in high glee. To see such a contest took him back to his boyhood days, and he half wished he was in the race himself.

Both reached the rock at precisely the same time, and rested heavily on it for a second, so that Barringford might see that it was really and truly "teched," as he expressed it. It was somewhat over their heads, and in the water at their feet they could feel the sprawling roots of the tree behind it.

Then, exactly how it happened would be hard to tell, but without warning the great rock suddenly slipped from the river bank and went into the water with a loud splash, carrying the two swimmers down under it!

Barringford saw the catastrophe and for the instant he stood spellbound. It was as if the light of day had suddenly given way to the darkness of night. Both of his young friends were gone, carried to the bottom by that huge rock which had seemed such a safe point for the turn in the race.

The old frontiersman waited a few seconds—to him they seemed an eternity—and then, as neither Henry nor Dave reappeared, he plunged hastily into the river and swam in their direction with all his might and main. He was a good swimmer, and now desperation lent strength to his muscles.

He was in midstream when he saw a head bob up, and an instant later he recognized Henry. The youth was panting for breath.

"Henry!" he called out. "Henry! Whar is Dave!"

"I—I—don't know!" came with a gulp and a gasp. "That rock was—was almost the de—death of me!"

"Dave must be under it!" groaned the old frontiersman. "We must help him, or he'll be drowned!"

"Yes! yes!" Henry tried to catch his breath. "Oh, Sam, what shall we do?"

He tried to look down into the water, but the falling of the rock had dislodged a quantity of dirt also, and what had before been so clear was now muddy, so that little or nothing could be seen excepting the top of the stone, which now lay about six inches below the surface.

"Can't you see him at all?" queried Barringford, after a painful pause.

"I can't see anything. Oh, this is awful!"

"Dive an' take a look!" ordered the old frontiersman, and taking as good a breath as his condition would allow, Henry went down, to catch hold of the sprawling roots with his hands and try his best to locate the body of his cousin. But the muddy water made his eyes smart, and seeing was practically out of the question. More than this, the great rock was slowly sliding outward, to the deeper part of the stream, so he had to watch out for fear of being caught once more.

"Didn't see him?" asked Barringford, as he came closer.

"No, it's too rily."

"I'll go down myself."

Barringford was as good as his word, and went down without an effort, his water-soaked clothing aiding him to sink. He caught hold of the rock and the roots and strained his eyes in all directions. Then the rock began to move once more, and he had to get out of the way just as Henry had done.

"I'm afraid it's all up with the poor lad," he said, when he could speak. "If he's down there, he's drowned by this time."

"Don't let us give up, Sam," pleaded Henry, and started to go down once more, when the rock turned completely over, and a long tree root flew up close to the surface of the stream.

"There he is!" shouted Barringford, and swam forward. He was right, the tree root had brought up the body of Dave, and the young pioneer lay before them, his eyes closed and nothing giving any indication that he was still alive. Both swam to it, and in a second more they had it in their arms and were making for the shore with their burden.

CHAPTER XXIII

DAVE AND THE FAWN

"Sam, do you think he will live?"

Over and over Henry asked the question as he and the old frontiersman worked over the inanimate form they had brought to shore from the waters of the river.

"Hope so, Henry, but I can't tell yet," was Barringford's answer. "We'll do all we can, and trust the rest to God."

Both worked with a will, doing whatever they thought was best. Barringford held Dave up by the ankles and allowed much of the water to run from the unfortunate's mouth, and then they rolled the youth and worked his arms and rubbed him.

At first it looked as if all their efforts would be in vain, and tears gathered in Henry's eyes. But then they saw Dave give a faint shudder, followed by a tiny gasp.

"He's comin' around!" shouted Barringford, in a strangely unnatural voice. "Praise Heaven for it!"

But there was still much to do before Dave could breath with any kind of regularity, and they continued to rub him

Edward Stratemeyer

and slap him, while Barringford forced him to gulp down a small quantity of stimulants brought along in case of emergency. Then a fire was started up, and later on Henry brought over the youth's clothes, for to take Dave across the stream was out of the question.

For over an hour Dave felt so weak that neither of the others attempted to question him. Both helped him into his clothes, and gave him something hot to drink, and made him comfortable on a couch of twigs and leaves.

"I thought my time had come when I went under," he said, when he could talk. "The rock pinned me down between the tree-roots, and if it hadn't been for the roots, I suppose I should have been crushed to death. I held my breath as long as I could, and then I gulped in some water and lost my senses."

"It was truly a narrow escape," was Barringford's comment. "I didn't expect no sech accident when I let ye go into the swimmin' match."

"Did you go under, Henry?"

"Yes, but I soon got myself loose," was the reply. "I was almost scared stiff when you didn't come up, Dave. After this we'll have to be more careful than ever."

"It was wuss nor thet wildcat, I reckon," came from Barringford.

"I should say so," returned Henry promptly. "It almost makes me vow never to go in swimming again."

As Dave continued to feel weak it was decided to remain where they were all of the next day. Henry procured a log and some brushwood, and on these ferried over their things, and he likewise tied up the horses, so that they might not stray away.

By morning Dave felt more like himself, and he would have gone ahead on the hunt, but Barringford would not permit it.

"We have plenty of time," said the old frontiersman. "You jest lay around in the sun, an' you'll feel better for it."

"Well, then, you and Henry can go out," insisted Dave. "There is no reason why you should suck your thumbs waiting for me."

At this the others demurred, but about noon, having had a lunch, Barringford and Henry set out, promising to return before sundown. They had not expected to hunt on this side of the river, but, now they were there, the old frontiersman said they might see what they could stir up.

The camp had been pitched behind some bushes that fringed the river bank. Close at hand was a clump of trees, and back of these was the edge of the mighty forest, yet unspoiled by the ax of the pioneer. Not far from the camp was a small brook where the water rushed over a series of sharp rocks, making a murmur pleasing to hear.

Having straightened out the camp, Dave took Barringford's advice and lay down in the warm sunshine to rest. The little work that he had done had tired him more than he was willing to admit, and, having closed his eyes to do some thinking, he quickly fell into a sound slumber which lasted for several hours.

When he awoke all was still around him, and he rubbed his eyes, wondering what had aroused him. Then he caught sight of a tiny squirrel sitting bolt upright at the foot of the nearest tree, gazing curiously at him.

"Hullo, you little rascal!" said Dave, good-naturedly. "So you ran across me, did you? What kind of an animal did you take me for?"

The squirrel continued to gaze at him, but at his first movement to arise, the frisky animal gave a swish of his brush and was gone up the tree in a twinkling.

"Don't believe in making friends, that's sure." went on the young pioneer as he stretched himself. "Heigh-ho, but I must have slept pretty soundly, and for three hours at least! Well, it was as good a way as any to put in the time."

The sunshine had made Dave thirsty, and presently he walked to the brook to get a drink. As he was in no hurry he took his time, and, consequently, made little or no noise.

He had parted some low bushes, and was just looking for some favorable spot at which to bend down, when something caused him to look up the brook. There, to his astonishment and delight, he beheld a beautiful fawn, standing in several inches of water, watching some birds which circled close by.

"Oh, what a shot!" was Dave's thought, and as quietly as a mouse he fell back out of sight and then ran to where he had left his gun. The weapon was ready for use, and soon he was at the brook once more.

There was no breeze blowing, and the only sound that broke the stillness was the rushing of the little watercourse and the songs of half a dozen birds in the vicinity. The fawn was still there, but seemed to be on the point of running away; why, Dave could not tell.

Not to let such a chance to bag tender meat escape him, the young pioneer took hasty aim and fired. The bullet sped true, and, with a convulsive leap into the air, the fawn fell into the shallow brook dead.

While the smoke was still pouring from his gunbarrel, Dave caught sight of a larger deer, previously hidden from view by some brushwood. Scarcely had he laid the fawn low when another gunshot rang out, and this deer also went down, kicking convulsively.

"Hullo, Sam and Henry must be near!" he thought, and ran forward to make certain that the second animal should not get away. At the same time he set up a shout, so that neither of the others might fire on him by mistake.

But the second shot bad been almost as true as the first, and by the time he came up the large deer was breathing its last.

"Hullo!" he shouted. "We must have spotted these deer at exactly the same time."

No answer came back to this call, and now Dave looked around with surprise. If Henry and Barringford were near, why did they not show themselves?

"It's mighty queer," he muttered to himself. "If they—hullo! Hector Bergerac!"

Dave was right, and an instant later the French hunter and trapper stepped into the opening. He gazed around sharply to see if the young pioneer had any companions with him. His clothing was almost in tatters, and his general manner showed that he had been having a hard time of it.

"Are you alone, Morris?" was his first question.

"Perhaps I had better ask you that question," came just as quickly from the young pioneer.

"Yes, I am alone," was the answer. "I was making my way to your father's trading-post when I saw the deer and shot it."

"And I shot the fawn. What were you going to do at the trading-post?"

"I wish to talk to your father on matters of business."

"Did Jean Bevoir send you?"

At the mention of Bevoir, Hector Bergerac's face grew dark and took on a look full of bitterness.

"No, he did not send me, I came of my own accord. I was a fool to go with him in the first place, and that is why I wish to see your father."

"Did you have anything to do with the looting of the pack-train?"

"No! no! I am not a robber of the road, like Bevoir and Valette. They wanted me to go into the thing, but I refused. Then we quarreled, and I went my own way. But after that Jean Bevoir made me a prisoner—he and Flat Nose—thinking I was going to tell upon them. I was a prisoner until yesterday, when I managed to get away, taking this gun with me. For twenty-four hours I have tasted nothing but one little bird, and I am half starved."

"You say you want to see my father," went on Dave after a pause. "May I ask what you wish of him?"

"I want to tell him of some plans Bevoir and Flat Nose have made. They wish to make trouble."

"Are they near here?"

"No, they are going away for the present. But they will be back, either in the winter or the spring."

Hector Bergerac was willing enough to go into the camp with Dave, and between them they dragged the fawn and the large deer to the spot. The fire was started up and some venison set to broiling, and of this the Frenchman partook liberally, proving that he was indeed half starved.

"You cannot be alone," he ventured, while eating. "Where are your companions?"

"They are off on a hunt, but will soon be here," answered Dave; and half an hour later Barringford and Henry put in an appearance. They were doubly astonished, first upon seeing Bergerac and then upon seeing the game. Their own luck had not been very good, and they only had a few birds and a beaver to their credit.

They listened with interest to what Bergerac had to tell, and when the Frenchman had warmed up he related the full particulars of how Bevoir, Valette, and Flat Nose had concocted the plan to loot the Morris' pack-train, corroborating Glotte's story in all details. He said that all the Frenchmen with Bevoir knew that it was nothing but an act of thievery, but that some of the Indians had looked upon it merely as the beginning of the new uprising against the English, an uprising which he considered had been started by Pontiac and those under the great chief.

"I am no longer for war," he concluded. "I wish only for peace, and I am sorry that I did not remain in the St. Lawrence territory. The war has cost me all that I possessed. It was not much, but it was enough. Now I must start over again."

"If you will do what is square, my father will be glad to deal with you, and he will pay you all your skins are worth," returned Dave. "But you must not play him false."

"He can trust me, take my word upon it," said Hector Bergerac. "I have thought it over, and I feel certain that French rule in this country is at an end. England is too strong for us. To fight longer would be like striking one's head against a stone wall."

"Which shows that you have some sense," put in Barringford. "I must say I'm sick o' war too. Let us all go to huntin,' I say, an' make money. If the French an' the English would unite, we'd have nothin' to fear from the redskins."

"But they will not unite, it is not in their nature. But if they will only keep the peace, it will help greatly," concluded Bergerac.

He was worn out from traveling and glad enough to remain with the others over night. He dressed his deer and said he would take the skin to the trading-post, and also such a part of the meat as he could readily carry.

"He probably means to turn over a new leaf," said Henry, after Bergerac had departed. "I hope he does."

"He seemed to be mighty anxious to see your uncle," put in Barringford.

"Well, if he can save Uncle James from serious trouble, I hope he does it."

"What a scoundrel Jean Bevoir is!" put in Dave. "Wouldn't you think that, after all his upsettings, he would be content to rest and do what was right?"

"Some men are born that way, lad," said the old frontiersman. "It's in their nature. He won't stop bein' bad until he's
killed or dies a natural death; no two ways on't."

"I think Jacques Valette must be about as bad."

"More 'n likely—blackbirds generally flock together. But I
don't reckon that Valette is the schemer Bevoir is—he don't
keep sober enough."

"I've often wondered if it wasn't Bevoir who robbed Valette
that time." ventured Dave. "I think he'd be equal to it."

"Like as not—or else Valette dropped his money on the trail
an' never knew it."

CHAPTER XXIV

SOMETHING ABOUT SLAVES
AND INDIAN CAPTIVES

Two days later found the young hunters and Barringford about forty miles further to the northwest of the trading-post, at one of the most beautiful spots it is possible to imagine.

To the westward was a small stream running silently through a wide stretch of prairie land, the banks covered with bushes and plants. To the eastward was the edge of the mighty forest, a few giant trees standing out picturesquely in the foreground. Under the trees lay the sprawling roots, covered in spots with light and dark green moss, as soft to tread upon as the richest velvet carpet. At one side of the camp was a small series of rocks, and from them gushed forth a spring of cold water, running over the rocks and into the tall grass out of sight.

The weather had remained perfect, and the last twenty-four hours had been productive of sport not to be despised. They had found a beaver dam and taken twelve beavers, and had also laid low two deer and a cougar, or panther. The last-named animal had been found asleep by Barringford, and a single bullet had dispatched it almost before the beast awakened.

"Thet's what I call dead-easy huntin'," Barringford remarked when the panther was found to be dead. "No fight nor nuthin'."

"You won't often surprise the game like that," replied Henry.

The two young pioneers had surveyed the panther with interest. The fur, even at this season of the year, was fairly good, and they had assisted Barringford in dressing it, and it now hung on a branch of the nearest tree.

"What a farm one could have here," declared Dave, as his eye roved over the stretch of prairie. "Not a single tree to cut down or stump to burn or drag out."

"And just look at the soil," came from Henry. "As black and rich as any I ever saw. A fellow could raise anything he wished without half trying."

"It is certainly beautiful ground," put in Barringford, who sat in the shade, smoking a red clay pipe with a reed stem. "An' some day you'll see a plantation here true enough."

"How well the Indians could live, if they would only till this soil," continued Dave. "But you can't get them to raise anything but a little maize and tobacco."

"They are natural-born hunters—just like I am," said Henry with a short laugh.

"Sam, shall we find that buffalo we've been talking about?"

The old frontiersman blew a long stream of smoke from his mouth ere replying. "Will it rain afore Sunday, Dave?" he drawled.

"What has that got to do with it?"

"Nuthin'; only you know as much about thet as I do about the buffalo. Ef he comes this way, we'll git him, an' if he don't, why, we won't git him, thet's all," and the old frontiersman continued his enjoyment of the pipe.

"You said buffaloes like such prairie ground as this," declared Henry.

"So they do, so they do; but most of the buffaloes thet war here air gone—either killed, or lit out to the westward. Ye see," went on the old hunter, "buffaloes air like elk—they need lots o' elbow-room. I've been told thet a young buffalo will travel fifty miles an' think nuthin' of it."

"I don't think I want to try running down a young one then," answered Henry. "I'll try an old one that can't travel over three or four miles," and this caused a general laugh.

They had spent the entire morning on the edge of the prairie, keeping somewhat out of sight so as not to disturb any game that might appear. All had enjoyed an unusually hearty dinner, and were quite content to take it easy during the middle of the day. A faint breeze was blowing which was exceedingly pleasant, for the morning had been a trifle warm.

"I wonder what the folks are doing just now," mused Henry.

"I think I can tell you," answered Dave. "Your father and Rodney are getting ready to go back to the field to work, your mother is clearing off the table, and little Nell is playing with the twins. Perhaps they are wondering what we are doing at the trading-post, too."

"Them twins is what gits me," came from Barringford. "It's mighty funny I can't find out who they belong to, ain't it?"

"It is in one way, Sam; but you must remember that many women and children have been lost in the last five or six years. This war has been simply awful in that respect. The Indians don't think anything of carrying them off into captivity."

"Well, why should they, when you come to think of it?" came from Henry.

"Oh, Henry!"

"Now, hold on, Dave, let me reason it out for you. The whites hold hundreds of black slaves, don't they?"

"Yes."

"Well, to an Indian it is no worse for a red man to hold a white person as a captive than it is for a white man to own a slave. It's a poor rule that won't work both ways."

"The blacks are naturally slaves—ain't good fer nuthin' else," put in Barringford, who had some old-fashioned ideas on the subject.

"I don't believe that, Sam," came from Dave. "Some black people are wiser than you think. If they had the chance to rise, they'd do it."

"I heard tell that some men believe in freeing the blacks," came from Henry.

"Some on 'em don't want to be free," said the old frontiersman. "Jest look at the slaves belongin' to old Lord Fairfax, and to the Dinwiddies, and to the Washingtons.

Why, they all think it is an honor to belong to them families. They wouldn't go if ye druv 'em away."

"Yes, I know, for I have talked to some of 'em myself," said Dave. "The Washington blacks are particularly faithful. If they were set free I don't suppose they'd know what to do with themselves."

"They'd starve," said Barringford.

"But to come back to where we started from," went on Dave. "There is a difference between being a white man's slave and being an Indian captive. The whites don't kill their slaves or torture them."

"They torture some of 'em," replied Henry. "I've seen a negro whipped till it made my blood boil. Of course the majority of 'em are treated fairly good."

"A darkey who has a good home on the plantation has nuthin' to complain on," said Barringford. "His master feeds him, clothes him, and takes care of him when he's sick. In nine cases out of ten he's better off nor he would be if he had to shift fer himself."

"I shouldn't wonder if we had trouble some day over this slave question," came from Henry. "If they bring too many over, the slaves may rise up some day and try to wipe the whites out."

"Don't you fear for thet, Henry; they ain't equal to it, nohow."

"But if they join with the Injuns?"

"They'll never do thet nuther, an' you know it. A good darky ain't got no opinion at all o' a redskin—they hate 'em wuss nor p'ison."

How long the fruitless discussion might have lasted there is no telling, but during a brief pause Henry chanced to glance across the prairie and uttered an exclamation.

"Something is moving yonder. What is it?"

Barringford leaped to his feet and gave a long, earnest look.

"Buffaloes!" he said laconically. "Two on 'em!"

"Can we catch them?" queried Dave.

"We can try, lad. But keep under cover. They seem to be coming this way."

All three hurried back to the foremost trees in the forest, carrying their guns as they did so. Luckily the camp-fire had died out, so there was no smoke to alarm the animals. Further in the forest the horses were tethered, having had their fill of grass two hours before.

"Better see if the horses are ready for use, Henry," said Barringford. "We may have to do some tall riding for our game."

"I will," answered Henry, and ran back without loss of time. The three steeds were quickly saddled, and then the young hunter brought them forward in a bunch, still, however, keeping them out of sight of the prairie.

It was now seen that the buffaloes were indeed moving in the direction of the camp. The two that had at first appeared were followed by eight or ten others, who kept in a bunch several rods behind the leaders.

Edward Stratemeyer

"Oh, what a chance for big game!" whispered Dave. "If only we had two or three guns apiece!"

"Never mind, we have our pistols," came from Henry. "They'll count for something at close quarters."

"Whatever you do, don't all fire at once," cautioned Barringford. "One bullet may not be enough for one of the buffaloes. I'll fire first, and if he don't fall then Henry can fire, and then Dave."

Anxiously they waited for the big game to come within gun shot. The buffaloes moved slowly, and to Dave it appeared an age before even half the distance was covered.

"Oh, pshaw! They are turning to the northward!" cried Henry a few minutes later.

"Wait, they may turn this way again," said Barringford, but they were disappointed; the buffaloes continued to move in a direction that was parallel to the edge of the forest.

"We'll lose them unless we ride after them," said Dave; and a minute later all were in the saddle, leaving their camping outfit behind them.

They kept well in among the trees, riding as hard as possible, until half a mile was covered. Then Barringford slipped to the ground and crawled forward to the open.

"We are gaining on 'em," he announced. "Another ride like thet an' we can go after 'em on the prairie."

Once more they urged their steeds forward. The way was full of rocks and dangerous tree-roots, but the horses were growing used to such traveling and rarely made a misstep.

Twice they crossed little creeks which flowed into the larger stream beyond. Then, without warning, they reached a portion of the forest so thick with young trees that further progress in that direction was impossible.

"Nothing left but to take to the open and ride like the wind," announced the old frontiersman. "Are ye ready, lads?"

"Yes," came from both.

"Then follow me!"

Barringford turned his horse toward the open prairie, and the others came close behind him. Away they went at what to an ordinary observer would have seemed a breakneck speed. The little ride through the forest had warmed up the horses, and the rest of the morning had put them in fine condition for a good run. On they sped, as if they enjoyed it fully as much as did their riders.

"Don't make any noise," came from Barringford. "The nearer we get without bein' discovered the better."

At least a third of the distance toward the buffaloes was covered when suddenly the herd stopped short. They had heard the dull thud of the horses' hoofs, and now looked around to see what the sound meant. Then came a wild snorting and throwing of shaggy heads, and away went the herd due west and making the best speed of which their sturdy limbs were capable.

"They have found us out!" shouted Barringford. "Now to catch 'em—or miss 'em!"

"I don't intend to miss 'em," came warmly from Henry. "But I think you ought to give me the first shot if I get nearest to 'em."

"All right, Henry, so be it."

No more was said, for, with the pace such a hot one, nobody cared to waste breath in conversation. Far ahead the buffaloes were running as gamely as ever, being spread out somewhat in a semicircle, with the leader, a heavy old fellow with an extra shaggy head, a little in advance.

Slowly, but surely, Henry gained on both of his companions. His steed was the best of the three, and if Henry was a natural-born hunter and trapper he was likewise a good horseman. Bending low over the horse's neck he spoke words of encouragement, to which the animal responded to the best of his ability.

Thus mile after mile was covered, and still the buffaloes kept on as before. They were now coming to a locality where the prairie was broken up into little hummocks, with here and there gopher holes that were exceedingly dangerous.

At last all three of the hunters saw one of the buffaloes go down. One leg had gone into a gopher hole and become broken, and although the animal arose and tried to run, it was soon overtaken by Henry.

"Finish him off, Dave!" yelled back the young hunter. "I'm going to see if I can't run down another!" And he kept on as before.

Dave heard the cry. He could not make out what was said, but he understood, and riding up close to the hurt buffalo, he let the animal have a bullet directly in the head. It was a fair shot, and with a lurch the beast staggered a few feet and then fell with a heavy thud on the prairie.

"Good for you, Dave!" cried Barringford. "That makes number one. Now let us finish him and see if we can run down some more on 'em."

Edward Stratemeyer

CHAPTER XXV

THE RESULTS OF A BUFFALO HUNT

The brief stop made by Dave and Barringford had allowed Henry to increase his lead until now he was almost out of sight of those behind him. The prairie was growing rougher, and soon the buffaloes reached a small creek, bordered in spots with trees and brushwood. Into the creek they plunged boldly and scrambled up the opposite bank. Henry came after them, and now another level stretch of prairie was encountered at least a mile across and several times that in length.

The buffaloes were gradually turning to the northward once more, and by keeping straight for them Henry cut off much of the distance he would otherwise have been compelled to cover. He soon saw that they had changed their course because of a river they were afraid to swim, for it was shallow and the mud on the bottom was sticky and treacherous.

"They certainly know what they are doing," thought the young hunter. "Go along, Buzzy! We must catch them somehow!"

Buzzy heard the words and leaped forward in a fresh effort. As he did this Henry looked behind him, and was surprised to learn that both Dave and Barringford were nowhere in sight.

"Can they have given up the chase?" he asked himself. It was possible, but not at all probable. "Perhaps they had more trouble with that fallen buffalo than they expected," he thought.

At last Henry saw that the animals ahead of him were beginning to slacken their speed. The leader still kept on with three or four others, but the rest were dropping further and further behind. One in particular, quite a big beast, too, lagged more than any of them, and Henry soon spotted this for his own.

"I'll have you yet, old fellow," he told himself, and looked to see if the priming of his gun was still as it should be.

Once more the buffaloes made a turn to the westward, following the bank of the river just mentioned. The beast Henry had picked out was a dozen or more rods to the rear, and this distance was increasing rapidly. Evidently his wind had given out. Suddenly he stopped short, whirled around, and made straight for the young hunter!

Henry was not taken greatly by surprise, and had been on the lookout for such a trick. As the buffalo came closer he pulled the hammer of his gun. To his chagrin the weapon refused to go off, acting exactly as it had done when he was after the big elk.

"What luck!" he muttered, and then had to pull his horse to one side. The animal was now nervous, and in a twinkling it balked and sent Henry flying headlong to the ground! Then, without waiting to note what was happening, the horse set off on a run whence it had come.

Edward Stratemeyer

To face an angry buffalo had been bad enough while on horseback, but on foot it was doubly perilous. For the instant after he picked himself up Henry knew not what to do. Then, in sheer desperation, he raised his rifle once more and pulled the trigger as before.

The weapon now spoke up and the bullet hit the bison (for such the American buffalo really is) fairly and squarely between the eyes. Down went the beast as if struck with a heavy club. But the skull was thick and the shot was by no means fatal.

As soon as the gun was empty Henry retreated. He knew better than to use his pistol until it became absolutely necessary to do so. With all possible speed he reloaded the larger weapon.

The young hunter was just fixing the priming and looking to the flint when the bison came up with a snort and charged as before. There was blood trickling down his face and he presented a truly ferocious sight. Henry waited until the beast was but a few paces away, then aimed for the right eye once more and fired.

This time both gun and aim did not disappoint him. The bullet passed into the very brain of the buffalo, and he pitched over with a thud that could be heard for a long distance. Once or twice he pawed the prairie grass, but that was all.

Henry did not examine his prize at once. A glance convinced him that he had nothing more to fear in that direction, and then he looked for the other buffaloes. All were out of sight. He reloaded his gun and then began to search for his horse.

To his chagrin the steed was also among the missing, nor

could he catch sight of the animal anywhere, try his best. Then he looked for Dave and Barringford. They had not come up, and where they were there was no telling.

He was alone on the broad prairie with the dead buffalo. More than this, the chase had occupied considerable time, and he saw with some alarm that both night and a storm were coming up. Already in the west dark clouds were beginning to crawl up toward the orb of day. In a few minutes more the sun was obscured, and the bright stretches of the prairie took on a somber tone.

"Well, I'm certainly in a pickle," he thought. "I wonder where that horse went to, and how long it will be before Dave and Sam come up?"

Had there been a tree handy, Henry would have mounted it to take observations. But not even a hillock was near, and he had to content himself with remaining on the level, using his eyes to the utmost.

"If they don't come soon, I suppose I'll have to spend the night here," he mused. "That won't be very pleasant, especially if any wolves happen to be around."

Hoping every minute that Dave and Barringford would appear, Henry examined the dead buffalo. The prize was a big one, and it must be admitted that the young hunter was much elated as he surveyed it.

"For a first buffalo, I'm sure that isn't so bad," he thought. "The folks at home will be surprised when they hear about it."

Swiftly the storm came closer, and presently the scattering drops of rain came down, followed by a steady shower. With nothing to protect him, he was soon wet to the skin.

Knowing there was scant danger of a prairie fire during a storm, Henry took out his hunting-knife and cut up a small portion of the buffalo. Then he dug out the dry grass from under the game, lit his tinder-box, and started up a fire, feeding it both with grass and with some buffalo fat. The latter made quite a heavy smoke, and he hoped that this would attract the attention of the others.

But when fully an hour had gone by, Henry grew both hungry and uneasy. "Something serious must have happened," he mused. "They wouldn't leave me like this."

He set up a yell, using the utmost power of his strong lungs for that purpose. Only the patter of the rain answered him.

Crouching over the tiny fire, he cooked himself a bit of the buffalo meat and ate it. Then he walked over to the river and procured a drink. On every side he could see nothing but the prairie, with the stream running through it like a huge serpent. Close to the water's edge were a few bushes, and some of these he pulled up with ease, with which to replenish the fire.

To tell the truth, Henry felt very lonely. Often had he been out in the forest at night, but the present experience was new to him. Had there been some rocks at hand, or a single tree, he might have made himself feel at home, but this immense stretch of flat land, water-soaked and becoming fast wrapped in the darkness of night, was truly depressing.

"Give me the woods every time, for an outing," he said to himself. "But, now I am here, I reckon I've got to make the best of it."

Returning to the river, he pulled up what was left of the bushes. These he did not put on the fire, but propped up against the broad back of the buffalo, forming a little shelter, into which he crawled in an endeavor to protect himself from the rain. Night was now on him, and he felt certain that he would have to remain in the spot until morning.

"One thing is certain, I'll never forget this buffalo hunt," he murmured as he turned in. "It's not proving as much fun as I thought it would be."

For a good two hours Henry crouched in the little shelter, trying his best to go to sleep. The rain continued to come down, but fortunately it was not cold, so he suffered but little discomfort on that account. At last his head fell forward on his breast and he became oblivious to all around him.

Towards one o'clock in the morning the rain ceased and a brisk wind came up from the southwest. As the stars began to show themselves, the wind carried to the keen nostrils of several wolves the scent of the buffalo carcass. The wolves were hungry, and with little yelps of satisfaction they trotted off toward where the game lay.

It did not take the beasts long to get within a dozen yards of the dead buffalo. Several were about to leap forward to plunge their fangs into the cut flesh, when they made the discovery that a human being was present. At once a howling of dismay arose on the night air.

The howl awoke Henry with a start. For the moment he could not imagine what had awakened him, but, with the true instinct of the hunter, he reached for his gun and also felt to see if his hunting knife was where it should be.

"Wolves," he told himself, and set up a sudden yell. At the sound of his voice the beasts retreated into the darkness and began to yelp violently. They were much disappointed, for

Edward Stratemeyer

they had expected to have a rare feast on the big carcass lying before them.

"I'll have to stir up that fire, that's certain," thought the young hunter, and he made haste to use his tinder-box. But grass and bushes were too wet to ignite, and in a few minutes he had to give up the idea.

In the meantime the wolves had ranged themselves in a semicircle before him, continuing to howl as dismally as ever. One especially large beast came a little forward, showing his fangs viciously.

"Get back there!" cried Henry, and the leader of the wolves retreated for the moment. But then he came closer than ever, and the others followed.

Picking up one of the bushes, Henry threw it at the pack and all set up a wild yelping. Away they sped into the darkness, and he fancied they were gone. But this did not last. They came back howling with additional loudness, and drew closer and closer, until it looked as if the largest would certainly leap for the young hunter's throat.

Henry waited no longer, but, raising his musket, fired at the leader of the wolves. With a snarl the beast sprang into the air and whirled over and over in his death agonies. The struggle carried him further away from where Henry stood, and without loss of time the youth reloaded his weapon, so that he might be prepared for another attack.

The sudden fall of the leader disconcerted the other wolves for the time being, and it was fully five minutes before they came forward as before. Henry half expected them to eat the dead wolf, but they did not touch the body.

"Reckon they mean business," thought the young hunter,

setting his teeth hard. "They want either the buffalo or me! And they shan't have either—if I can help it!"

He yelled once more at the beasts, but this time they merely halted, showing that the sound of his voice did not alarm them as it had previously done. Then, like a flash, one leaped for Henry's throat.

Crack! went the rifle again, and this wolf also fell, shot through the throat. The wound was serious, but not fatal, and with gleaming teeth and eyes that blazed with fury the beast gathered himself for another spring. On he came, but Henry knew enough to leap to one side. Not wishing to use his pistol, excepting as a last resort, he drew his hunting-knife, and, watching his chance, plunged it into the wolf's shoulder. Down went the beast, and a second stroke of the blade finished the creature.

Scarcely was the second wolf down when all the others appeared to come forward in a bunch. Bang! went Henry's pistol, and a third wolf was struck in the breast. Then the youth caught up a bush and whirled it into the beasts' faces. But some got behind him, and one snapped at his hunting-shirt and another at his leather leggings. It looked as if in another minute he would be down and killed.

CHAPTER XXVI

STRANGE INDIAN MAGIC

"Well, where in the world can Henry have ridden to?"

It was Dave who asked the question. He sat on his horse, peering forth in all directions through the storm and the oncoming darkness. Beside him was Barringford, equally anxious to learn what had become of their companion.

Killing the first buffalo had not proved easy, and they had spent more time over the game than they had anticipated. But a bullet from Dave's pistol had finished the big creature, and then the pair had looked around for Henry, to find that he had vanished.

A hunt had followed in first one direction and then another. As the storm came up Dave's horse was unfortunate enough to run into a mud reach close to the river, and it proved no light task to save the steed from being drowned.

With the coming of night, Barringford had proposed that they go into camp, but Dave was too worried to do this, and urged that the search be continued.

"For all we know, those buffaloes may have turned and charged on Henry," he said. "I shan't rest until I know the truth."

"If they turned an' charged, I'm afeered it's all up with Henry." returned the old frontiersman. "A mad buffalo can make short work o' a hunter. He's wuss nor a mad bull."

They moved off slowly after this in something of a semicircle. Occasionally one or the other would raise a yell, but to these cries no answer was returned.

"Might as well give it up, Dave, onless ye want to ride around all night," said Barringford at last.

He had hardly spoken when Dave drew up his horse.

"Hark, Sam! what is that?"

The old frontiersman listened attentively for several minutes.

"Wolves, onless I miss my guess," he replied presently.

"They appear to be heading toward us."

"No, they are off in that direction, Dave." Barringford pointed with his hand. "They are after something."

"Not our buffalo meat, I hope."

"No, they are heading the other way. It's something else."

"Let us follow. They may be after another buffalo, or after Henry."

"That is so."

On they went once more. Soon they could no longer hear

the wolves, and drew up in perplexity. While they were consulting together, they heard a distant gun shot.

"Somebuddy is a-firin' on 'em!" ejaculated Barringford. "Perhaps it's Henry. Come!" And he set off at a gallop, with Dave beside him. As they rode on they heard another gun shot, and a moment later the report of a pistol.

"It must be Henry, and, if so, he is having a fearful fight with the wolves!" cried Dave. "Oh, Sam, we must help him!"

"I see him!" shouted Barringford, and in less than half a minute later he was blazing away at the wolves. Dave also fired his gun and his pistol, and four wolves were put out of the fight in almost the time it takes to tell of the deed.

"Save me!" came faintly from Henry. "Save me!"

"I will!" answered Barringford, and leaped from his horse, hunting-knife in hand. The blade was plunged deeply into a wolf that had Henry by the left arm. Dave used his musket as a club, and another of the beasts was sent staggering back with a broken jaw.

What few remained of the beasts were scared by the new arrivals, and now they made off at top speed. It was high time, for Henry had suffered much, and as soon as the living wolves had disappeared he plunged forward and fainted in Barringford's arms.

"He has had a tough time of it, poor fellow," murmured the old frontiersman. "If we hadn't 'a' come up as we did, he would have been done for."

"Is he seriously hurt?" questioned Dave anxiously.

"Don't think he is, Dave. It's his wind as has given out."

Barringford was right, and it was not long before Henry revived. His arm was slightly pierced in three places and on his left leg were two long, irregular scratches. These were washed and bound up by Dave, and during the time consumed Barringford managed to start up a tiny fire in spite of the dampness.

"Where in the world have you been?" asked Henry. "I watched and watched for you."

"And we've been hunting for you until we were about ready to give it up," answered his cousin. "The wolves put us on the track."

Sitting around the fire, which Barringford coaxed into a respectable blaze, each party told what had happened since the separation.

"Reckon as how you've had your fill o' buffalo huntin' jest for the present," said Barringford, when the narratives were concluded. "Buffaloes an' wolves is a terribul bad combination."

"Where is your game?" questioned Henry.

"About two mile from here, I reckon."

"Perhaps the wolves will be after that."

"Can't help it if they air, lad. Dave wanted to look for you, an' wouldn't stay by the game nohow. Can't blame him, nuther, seein' as we came up jest in the nick o' time," added the old frontiersman.

All thoughts of sleep were now out of the question, and the

three sat around the tiny campfire, discussing the situation. With the first streak of dawn Barringford set to work skinning the buffalo, and Dave assisted.

While they were thus occupied, Henry saw a familiar form advancing slowly over the prairie. He set up a call, and in a few minutes his horse came up on a trot, to mingle with the other horses.

"You rascal! to leave me in the lurch!" cried Henry, but he did not strike the steed, but patted him instead. "Be thankful that he has come back," said Barringford. "Sometimes a frightened critter like thet runs off an' never shows himself again." After the buffalo had been skinned, the best portions of the meat were cut out and rolled in the hide, which was strapped to the back of Barringford's saddle. The wolves were left where they had fallen. "Sooner or later them other wolves will come back," said the old frontiersman, "an' they'll eat wot's left of the buffalo an' the wolves' carcasses, too." It was fully an hour before they reached the spot where the other buffalo had fallen. No wild beasts had been near the carcass, and now this was also dressed and the hide packed up behind Dave. Then they set off for the camp on the edge of the prairie, reaching it shortly after noon. "I declare, the spot seems like home!" cried Dave. "I must say I am glad to return to it." All were equally happy, and lost no time in preparing a regular meal, which tasted far better than the makeshift they had indulged in early in the morning. Hunting was declared to be at an end for the time being, and for the rest of that day, and all of the next, the three took it easy.

"My bear hasn't shown himself," said Dave. "But I reckon I can do without him."

The rest of the hunting tour passed without anything out of the ordinary happening. Many small animals were brought in by both Dave and Henry, and Barringford varied the sport by laying low a wildcat that came one night to rob them of some of the meat.

When the start for the trading-post was begun, they found their steeds loaded down with the trophies of the chase. Consequently, progress was slow, and it took one day longer than they had expected to reach the Ohio.

"Back again, I see!" cried James Morris cheerily. "And safe and sound, too! I am glad to see it."

"We've had a powerfully good trip," answered Barringford. "Two buffalo, an' no end o' small game."

"That is certainly fine. Boys, I reckon you are proud of the haul."

"We are," answered Dave promptly, and Henry nodded. "Have you seen anything of Hector Bergerac?" he continued.

"Yes, he is here now. He has told me his story, and told me all about Jean Bevoir, Jacques Valette, and that redskin they call Flat Nose. Hector Bergerac wants to cut the whole crowd, and I am going to help him to do it."

The weather had threatened a change, and inside of a week after Dave and his companions returned to the trading-post there was a heavy frost, and, two days later, a touch of ice.

"I think winter is coming now," said James Morris. "And if anybody is going to start for home he'll have to do it soon."

"I shouldn't mind taking the trip," answered Dave. "It seems an age since I saw Uncle Joe and the others."

The matter was talked over for several days, and it was finally agreed that Dave should go eastward this time, in company with Barringford and White Buffalo and his braves. Henry would remain with his uncle, and so would the others at the trading-post. Only a few horses were to be taken along, and in the spring Dave and Barringford were to purchase ten additional steeds, and bring along a well-guarded pack-train containing goods to the value of eight hundred pounds. The trading-post was now doing well, and it looked as if, sooner or later, the Morrises would make a small fortune out of it.

The departure was made in a keen, frosty air, which was as clear as it was invigorating. Henry and Dave's father accompanied those who were going as far as the burn-over on the Kinotah, and then watched them out of sight around a bend of the trail.

"It looks a bit familiar to me now," said Dave to Barringford, as they rode along under the big trees.

"I suppose in a few years more there will be a regular road here, just as there now is from Fort Pitt eastward."

"Like as not, lad, onless the redskins upset everything again."

"They have been very quiet lately."

"Yes, Dave, but thet may be the calm afore a storm, as sailor men call it. I don't believe in trustin' a quiet Injun."

"White Buffalo is good enough when he is quiet," answered the youth, with a merry glance at the chief mentioned, who was riding a short distance to the rear.

"True, but a few good Injuns don't make a basketful,"

answered Barringford, using a form of speech he had heard once when down East.

The weather proved fine until Fort Pitt was gained. Here the party put up for two days, the commandant of the stronghold being glad to meet those who might bring news.

"All is quiet here," said the officer. "There was something of a plan to attack us during the summer, but it fell through, why I don't exactly know. I think the Indians are waiting for the French to help them."

"Will they do that?" asked Dave.

"I don't think so. The French are having their hands full in the old country."

When the party left Fort Pitt the sky was overcast, and that night came a light fall of snow. They had been told that there had been a landslide on the route, and that they had better take another trail, one leading around to the northward.

"This trail bring party to Indian village of Ninalicmic," announced White Buffalo.

"Are they much of a tribe?" asked Dave.

"Only a handful. But my white brothers must beware of the Ninalicmics. They are of the magicians, and do great wonders."

"They are a branch of the magicians who live up near the lakes," put in Barringford. "I've heard of them, but I thought they had cleared out long ago."

When they came close to the village, they heard a strange

Edward Stratemeyer

beating of Indian tom-toms and a loud shouting and clapping of hands.

"Some kind of dance going on," said Barringford. "Reckon as how I'll go in advance and see if it's safe to break in on 'em."

"Let me go with you," said Dave.

The others were halted, and Dave, Barringford, and White Buffalo went forward on foot, keeping themselves out of sight behind a row of bushes and a series of low rocks.

Before them was a fair-sized glade, in the midst of which was located the Indian village, consisting of a dozen or more wigwams, all of good dimensions and each gaudily painted with many signs and symbols. In front of several of the wigwams were erected posts on which hung strips of feathers and other strips of bear's claws and wampum belts that were new to Dave's eyes.

In the center of the village was a cleared space, and here a bright campfire was burning. On each side sat several Indians, all smeared with various colored paints and greases. Other red men were dancing around the fire, keeping time to the tom-toms and chanting in a low, monotonous tone.

"Big medicine men and magicians," said White Buffalo. "Make much magic."

Dave looked at his old Indian friend and saw, to his astonishment, that White Buffalo was ill at ease, if not actually nervous. Had he been alone, it is likely that he would have turned on his heel and hurried away.

"What be they a-saying?" demanded Barringford, after listening to the chant. "I never heard sech gibberish in my life afore."

"Much magic," answered White Buffalo. "Magic make the Indians strong to fight their white enemies."

"Oh, so that's it, eh? Do they believe in it, White Buffalo?"

"Magic is magic," returned the old chief simply.

"Does it mean digging up the war hatchet?"

"White Buffalo cannot tell, for he is not in their secrets. But if the hatchet should be dug up—ha!"

White Buffalo stopped short, for the flap of one of the wigwams had opened and a tall Indian had stepped outside. The red man was naked to the waist and painted with rings and blotches of several colors. On his head he carried something of a crown of black feathers with brass ornaments dangling over each ear. As he came out, those around the fire set up a yell of welcome.

"Who is it?" questioned Dave, in a whisper.

"Pontiac, the great chief of the Ottawas," answered White Buffalo. And then he added hastily, as Pontiac threw up his arms and swept them around in a circle: "Let us go, let us not stay! It is not safe! Pontiac will make great magic! Let us go ere it is too late!"

CHAPTER XXVII

THE TRAIL OF PONTIAC

The fright of such a brave chief as White Buffalo may seem strange to my young readers, but it must be remembered that among the Indians the art of magic was considered the blackest art of all, and a magician was looked upon as something far out of the ordinary. The art was somewhat similar to that of the voodoos of the South, and the fakirs of India, and a real magician was looked up to and obeyed where a common medicine man would be ignored.

It is said, upon fairly good authority, that Pontiac belonged to the magicians of the Great Lakes. This has already been mentioned, but nothing has been said of how he practiced the black art. Much that was recorded has been lost, so some things can only be surmised. But his doings had a strong hold on all who came in contact with him, making his friends stick to him closer than ever, and causing many of his enemies to drop their antagonism and sue for peace.

"Don't you get afraid of him, White Buffalo," whispered Barringford. "His magic is all humbug."

"No! no! it is true!" insisted the Indian chief. He caught Dave by the hand. "Come! If Dave is caught watching, he will surely lose his life!"

"I shall stay, if Sam stays," said the youth. "We'll take good care that we are not discovered."

"You can go back to the others," went on Barringford. But at this White Buffalo demurred, and in the end remained to see the weird performance.

The dance of the magicians lasted fully a quarter of an hour. Then came a low chant, and a conference followed. Strange strings of beads were exchanged, and finally Pontiac made an address, in an Indian dialect of which neither Barringford nor Dave could understand a word.

White Buffalo listened to the address with keen interest. His first fright over, he was now fairly calm, and when Pontiac stopped and prepared to leave the village he pulled the others back to a place of safety.

"Pontiac will go away alone," he said. "White Buffalo follow on the trail. Want his brothers Dave and Sam to come, too."

"Why?" asked the others, in a breath.

"Learn much. Maybe do the English great good. Pontiac is like a fox in wisdom. If the spell of magic is broken, Pontiac may fall as falls the mighty tree of the forest before the hurricane."

"I must say I don't quite follow ye, Buffalo," came from Barringford. "Where is Pontiac going?"

"To the woods, where the waters fall in the sunshine. White Buffalo thinks he knows the spot, but he is not sure."

"Why should we follow him?"

"White Buffalo cannot explain. There is much magic. Perhaps the coming of night will clear the mystery."

Both Dave and Barringford were much perplexed. Never before had White Buffalo acted in this manner, and it was easy to see that he was laboring under great excitement.

"We may as well do what White Buffalo says," came from Dave, after he had talked to the old frontiersman in private. "We'll only lose a day or two by the operation and we are in no particular hurry to reach Will's Creek."

"Very well, lad, I'll go ye on't," was the answer. "We may learn something of great importance to the English authorities."

White Buffalo had by this time joined those of his tribe who were with him. His speech to his followers was as peculiar in its effects as had been the mysterious incantations of the magicians upon himself. Two voted to follow Pontiac, while the others said they would not do so under any circumstances. "The squaws can return to the trading-post," said the chief. And thus were the others dismissed. A short while after this all were on the trail of Pontiac, who, contrary to expectations, had taken with him a young brave known by the extraordinary name of Foot-in-His-Mouth, a Wyandot famous for his accuracy at shooting. Foot-in-His-Mouth had often won prizes at target shooting, both among the Indians and the French, and he was called one of the best hunters in the Ohio valley. Both Pontiac and his escort were on horseback, and they rode so swiftly along the forest trail that the others had all they could do to keep close to them. White Buffalo led, and never once did he allow those he was following to suspect his presence. Whenever they slowed up so did he, and instead of passing over an open space he invariably rode around it, keeping his steed in the shelter of the trees and brushwood. "If he is simply going to his home on the Detroit River, we'll have our ride for nothing," observed Dave, after six or eight miles had been covered.

"Oh, something is in the wind, you may be sure of that," returned Barringford. "The question is, what is it?"

It was growing dark when Pontiac and his companion came to the side of a fair-sized brook, rushing swiftly over some rough rocks. They passed up this brook for a distance of several hundred feet and then took to the other side. Here there was a burnt spot covering half an acre, and Dave and the others noted the remains of a cabin.

"Somebuddy lived here once an' was wiped out," remarked the old frontiersman laconically. "Can't tell who did it."

The falling of waters could now be plainly heard, and before long Pontiac and Foot-in-His-Mouth reached a beautiful waterfall, fifteen or eighteen feet in height. The fall was narrow and was lined upon either side with rugged rocks, overgrown with mosses and trailing vines. At the foot of the waterfall was a circular pool of great depth.

Pontiac and his companion came to a halt and, dismounting, tied their horses to trees near by. At once those who were following did the same, and all crawled forward with extreme caution to learn what would next take place.

For several minutes Pontiac stood talking earnestly to Foot-in-His-Mouth, and pointing to the waterfall. Then both climbed the rocks at the side of the fall until they could touch the water with their hands.

"Something is up now, that's certain!" whispered Dave.

The words had just been uttered when a curious thing

Edward Stratemeyer

happened. With a quick movement Pontiac stepped through the waterfall and disappeared from sight!

"Well, I never!" murmured Dave. "Where did he go to?"

"Hush!" murmured Barringford. "Look!"

Foot-in-His-Mouth was gazing fixedly at the waterfall. He hesitated for fully a minute. Then, watching his chance, he dove into the waterfall as Pontiac had done and also disappeared.

White Buffalo looked at his white companions gravely. "Do my white brothers know what that means?" he asked.

"I think I do," answered Barringford. "There must be a cave back there, and the opening to it is through the waterfall."

"But how would they be able to find such a cave?" questioned Dave.

"In two ways, lad. There may be some other opening, and they may have discovered this opening when the waterfall had run dry."

"It must be a cave," came from White Buffalo. "And if it is, it is the cave Pontiac told about at the village of Ninalicmic."

"What did he say about it?"

"Pontiac told of planting guns in the ground. He said they would grow, and the Indians could one day pluck them and use them."

"Planting guns? I don't understand."

"It's an amazement truly," put in Barringford. "We won't know what it means until—"

"Until what, Sam? Do you feel like following into the cave?"

"I shouldn't mind if I knew the directions Pontiac gave to that other redskin. But without them directions a feller might lose his life easy enough in the attempt. He might have told him to turn to the left or the right, or somethin' like that, you know."

"True enough. Well, what do you advise?"

The matter was talked over with White Buffalo, and it was decided to remain where they were until Pontiac and Foot-in-His-Mouth returned for their horses.

"They are bound to do thet, sooner or later," said Barringford. "By the way they tethered 'em I reckon they expect to come back shortly."

An hour passed, and Dave was growing tired of the watch, when White Buffalo, who lay beside him, gave his sleeve a quick jerk and nodded toward the waterfall. As the young hunter looked in the direction he saw a sudden movement, and Pontiac emerged on the rocks, dripping wet. An instant later Foot-in-His-Mouth followed, and both climbed down to the side of the pool.

"They have been on some sort o' a mission," whispered Barringford. "Wonder what's next?"

Untying their horses, Pontiac and his companion turned them up the slope leading to the stream above the waterfall. Here the pair consulted for some time. What was said neither White Buffalo nor those with him could make out. But soon Pontiac rode off in one direction and Foot-in-His-

Mouth in another.

"Shall we follow Pontiac further?" questioned Dave. "For my own part I'd rather stay here and find out what this cave, if such it is, contains."

"'Tis the cave of the magicians," answered White Buffalo. "My white brothers must be careful how they enter it."

"I am not afraid of magic, White Buffalo. But of course I want to know what I am doing."

"We can examine the place in the dark as well as the daylight," came from Barringford. "It's queer Pontiac and his friend didn't take torches with 'em."

"There may be torches inside."

"Perhaps; but if I go in I'll take my own torch."

"So will I, Sam, and a good big one, too."

Again there was a consultation, and at last it was agreed that Barringford should attempt to enter the cave first. If he succeeded, and the way was an easy one, Dave was to follow, and lastly White Buffalo. The other Indians would remain on guard.

Tucking a good bit of torch wood in his leathern belt, Barringford climbed up to the footing Pontiac had first occupied. He examined the waterfall with care and also looked at the pool below.

"Don't think I'll git more 'n a dirty tumble if I fail to git in," he said to Dave. "Here goes!"

He made a leap and passed through the falling sheet of

water before him. With his heart almost in his throat, Dave watched and waited. He was still doing this when suddenly Barringford came to view again.

"It's easy, boys," he chuckled. "Jest like walkin' down a pair o' big stone steps. Jump about six feet an' you'll be all right."

Again he passed through the waterfall, and now Dave and White Buffalo lost no time in following. The opening beyond was two feet wide and high enough for a man to stand upright. The flooring led downward several steps, and then turned to the left, where the passageway spread out into an irregular cave of uncertain dimensions and various heights.

"That was certainly easy enough," remarked Dave, while Barringford was busy lighting the tinder in his box. "I declare I only got the water on my head and shoulders. With a good big hood a fellow could keep as dry as a bone."

With some difficulty the tinder was lit and the torch followed. Swinging it around, Barringford soon had a good blaze, and then he held the torch aloft, that they might look around them.

Their first view of the interior of the cave was a disappointment. Close at hand were nothing but bare rocks, covered here and there with rude writing in the Indian language. A little further on were some heaps of bones, probably those of wild animals, but whether killed for the meat or not they could not tell.

"Not much wuth seein' so far," remarked the old frontiersman as he gave his torch another swing. "Let us move on."

Edward Stratemeyer

"Be careful, the walking may be treacherous," came from White Buffalo, and the warning came none too soon, for a short distance further on was an opening in the flooring a yard wide and of great depth. They leaped it with ease, but had one fallen into it there is no telling what would have happened.

Beyond this the passageway narrowed for a short distance. Here some of the rocks were wet, showing that there was a small stream or a pool of water overhead. The flooring was exceedingly rough, so that they had to move slowly and make sure of one footing ere they tried another.

"I wonder how long the Indians have known of this cave?" said Dave.

"White Buffalo hear of strange cave many years ago," came from the Indian chief. "Hear much when Colonel Washington and General Braddock fight the French and the Indians under Pontiac."

"Then is it a fact that Pontiac fought against us at that time?" asked Dave.

"White Buffalo has heard so. Pontiac is a great warrior."

"Hullo!" suddenly cried Barringford, who was a few feet in advance. "We're coming to something interesting now."

"What is it?" asked Dave eagerly.

"Look fer yourself, lad."

They had gained a portion of the cave that was almost circular in form. In the center was an immense black stone. On this rested a large pile of tobacco and several pipes, and beside these were strings of beads and wampum, and curiously shaped shells and spears. There were likewise some strings of feathers, and a dozen or more pairs of curiously worked moccasins. There were also a number of medals, evidently of English design and workmanship.

"Army medals!" cried Dave, picking one up. "Why, Sam, these must have been stolen from our soldiers!"

"Taken from our dead heroes most likely," answered the old frontiersman." It's a curious collection, ain't it, Dave?"

"Cave of the big council," said White Buffalo, pointing to the wampum strings and belts. "Much magic here."

"These are undoubtedly medals belonging to English soldiers and Royal Americans," said Dave, "They should be restored to their owners or else to the government."

"I agree with ye there, lad," answered Barringford. "An' when we leave we can take 'em along."

CHAPTER XXVIII

AN UNDERGROUND STOREHOUSE

To the Indians, as some of my young readers must know, many wampum belts were speech belts, usually given as a present when some great message was delivered. Consequently, White Buffalo looked the belts over with great interest, certain that they were connected with matters of great importance.

"Pontiac is as powerful as White Buffalo supposed," said he presently.

Dave and Barringford did not reply, for they had pushed on to another chamber of the cave. Here was an additional sight that made both cry out with wonder.

"Didn't expect nuthin' like this, did you, Dave?" queried Barringford.

"Not in the least," answered the young hunter.

The chamber was not very large, but it was literally filled with rifles and pistols of various sizes and makes, some still bright, and others much rusted from water and dampness. To the collection were added several swords, one with a scabbard and the others without. There were also a large number of powder horns and bullet pouches, and other soldier equipments.

"Where did all this stuff come from?" went on Dave. "It looks like part of an army outfit."

"Thet's jest wot it is, lad."

"And it must have belonged to our army."

"Right ag'in."

"If Pontiac was in command of the Indians at the time of General Braddock's defeat, do you suppose he had some of the red men bring this stuff here?"

"That's a question. Either the stuff came from thet place, or else from some other battle later on. One thing is sartin, there's a fairly good quantity on it and it ought to be restored."

"What had we best do—tell the commander at Fort Pitt?"

"I reckon thet would be the proper thing to do, Dave."

"I suppose Pontiac thinks to use these guns some day," went on the young pioneer. "He wanted to hide them until the time came to dig up the hatchet once more."

"White Buffalo's brother must be right," came from the Indian chief. "In a war the guns would give the Indians much power."

"Maybe Pontiac told the Indians he would make guns and swords by magic," said Dave suddenly.

"It is not impossible," returned White Buffalo gravely. "The magicians have brought forth powder by magic."

"And so can Pontiac!" shouted Barringford, who had moved to one corner of the chamber. "Reckon this is a bad place fer a torch," and he held back the flame,

"What have you discovered now, Sam?"

"Five half-kegs o' powder."

As he spoke the old frontiersman pointed to a rocky shelf whereon rested the five half-kegs, covered with a piece of heavy drugget, often used in colonial days in place of rubber cloth.

"Full too," said Dave, after lifting one. "Sam, this stuff is worth a good bit of money."

"Perhaps we'll git a reward if we return it to the government," was the answer.

"It ought to be returned, whether we get a reward or not."

"Exactly as I think."

There was a narrow passageway behind the chamber and Sam Barringford squeezed into this.

"Don't reckon I can make it," he panted presently. "Seems like I was a leetle too hefty. Dave, do you want to try it? Might be an opening to the outside world, an' if there is, we won't have to go through thet water ag'in."

Taking the torch, Dave pushed into the opening, which gradually grew smaller and smaller until he had to crawl on his hands and knees.

"Tight fit, eh?" called the old frontiersman after him.

"Yes, but it may be larger further on," answered the young pioneer, as he continued to advance.

Fortunately the passageway was dry, so he had nothing to fear from water. He progressed fully fifty feet, when he saw a large opening beyond.

"I'm coming to another room!" he shouted back.

But a sharp stone over a foot high barred his further progress. The stone appeared to be rather loose, and he fancied he could push it out ahead of him. Laying down the torch, he caught hold of the stone and soon had it turned from its resting place.

"What are you doing?" called Barringford.

"Getting a stone out of my way."

"You jest be careful how you loosen up these stones," returned the old frontiersman quickly. "The dirt don't seem to be none too hard, an'—"

Whatever else Sam Barringford said was lost upon Dave, for at that moment down came a quantity of dirt on the young pioneer which almost buried him. He attempted to back out the way he had come, but just as he was about to move, more dirt fell in that direction, followed by half a dozen large stones. Then, to avoid being completely caught, he pushed on ahead and by tight squeezing forced his way into the chamber beyond.

The fall of stones and dirt was as dismaying as it was perilous. Looking into the passageway, torch in hand, Dave saw that it was now completely choked. To get out by the

Edward Stratemeyer

way he had come was impossible. He was virtually entombed alive!

A shiver went over him and he called to Sam Barringford with all the power of his youthful lungs. To his intense dismay, no answer came back, showing that the fall of dirt and stones had been greater than anticipated.

"They'll surely try to dig me out," he thought. "But it may take a whole day, and in the meantime—"

He did not finish, but his heart sank within him. He examined the passageway once more and shouted as before. He fancied he heard an answer, but was not certain.

Looking about him, the young pioneer saw that he was in a cavern not over twenty feet square. Beyond was a tall split in the rocks which seemed to run upwards.

"That may lead to daylight," he thought. "Anyway, I might as well try it as stay here."

His torch was now burning so low he could no longer hold it. He looked around for something else with which to continue the light, but nothing was at hand. He rested the torch on a rock, and a few minutes later it fluttered up and went out, leaving him in total darkness.

It was a truly horrible situation and Dave's heart sank like a lump of lead in his bosom. For the time being all hope of escape appeared to be cut off. He shouted again and again, but could get no reply.

"Of course they'll do their best to dig me out," he reasoned, "but they have no tools, and the passageway was very small anyway. If the rocks are wedged in, all the power they can bring to bear won't budge them."

He felt around the chamber and soon found himself at the split in the rocks. He entered it for a distance of a few yards and then came back to the point from which he had started.

"It would be foolish to go into that in the dark," he thought. "I might fall into some ugly hole, or have worse luck. I'll stay here and see what comes."

He sat down and gave himself up to his reflections. They were rather bitter. He now realized how tired he was, and not long after this sank into merciful slumber.

When Dave awoke all was still dark around him. How long he had slept he could not tell, but he knew it must have been for some time, for he felt wonderfully refreshed. Getting up, he stretched himself, and his eyes roved around the chamber.

A single streak of light caught his eye, coming from the split he had failed to examine. He approached the split once more and saw that the light was stronger a short distance beyond, so strong in fact that he could see the surface of the rocks and dirt.

"It must be morning, and that must lead to the outer world," he told himself. "Can it be possible I have spent the whole night down here?"

The dampness had made him stiff in the joints, but to this he paid no attention. His one thought was to reach the top of the earth again. Feeling his way with care, he entered the split in the rocks and slowly climbed from one projection to another. The rocks came to an end amid the roots of a large tree, and in a few minutes more Dave was pulling himself up among the roots and into the open air.

The glorious sunshine struck full in his face as he emerged,

Edward Stratemeyer

to find himself on something of a sweeping hill, dotted here and there with trees and brushwood. His heart gave a leap for joy. Inwardly he thanked God for his safe deliverance from perils underground.

"Now to find my way back to the waterfall and let Sam and White Buffalo know that I am safe," he told himself. "But first I had better mark this spot, so that I can find it again."

With his hunting knife he started to make a blaze upon the tree. It was easily done, and he turned around to make certain of the locality.

Then, like lightning from a clear sky, came an attack as sudden as it was unexpected. Two forms leaped from behind some neighboring bushes. They were Indians and one held a tomahawk in his hand. With the flat of this he struck Dave a blow on the head, knocking him down.

"Don't!" gasped the young pioneer, when a second blow descended, giving him a shock he could not withstand. He stretched out his arms, and then rolled over on his back, senseless.

"'Tis one of the English," said the taller of the Indians, in his native language. "We were right to set a watch here."

"And what shall be done with him?" questioned the second. "Pontiac cares not for the scalp of a stripling."

"It shall be for Pontiac to answer," was the reply. "Bind him to yonder tree. There may be more to come forth, like foxes from their holes."

Without ceremony Dave's limp body was dragged into a thicket and fastened to a tree. Then the two Indians went back to renew their watch. This continued for the best part of an hour.

At the end of that time three other Indians appeared, including Foot-in-His-Mouth. The latter listened intently to what had happened.

"The fight is over," he said. "Two Indians are dead, and a white man and a Delaware squaw named White Buffalo have retreated in the direction of Fort Pitt. Let us away from here without delay, for I must report this new happening to Pontiac."

"And the stripling, what of him?"

"Bring him along."

Dave was just returning to his senses when the Indians shook him roughly. A scalping knife was brandished before his eyes, and he was given to understand that he must either walk with them or suffer death.

"Where are you going to take me?" he asked, when he felt strong enough to speak.

This question the Indians would not answer. But two of them shoved him roughly, and he was compelled to walk to where a number of horses were in waiting. With his hands tied behind him, and his head aching severely, he was mounted on one of the animals, and the entire party set off northward through the forest.

"If only Sam was here," thought the young pioneer dismally. He did not know that a fierce hand-to-hand conflict had taken place near the waterfall, and that Barringford and White Buffalo had barely escaped with their lives, yet such was a fact.

Edward Stratemeyer

The ride was a rough and hard one for Dave, and long before it came to an end he was ready to sink into a faint from exhaustion. Every time he reeled in the saddle one of the red men would shove him up roughly, or prick him with the end of a scalping knife.

At last the Indians called a halt at the foot of a small cliff. They dismounted and forced Dave to the ground, and the entire party ascended to the top of the cliff. Here was a well-defined path, and along this they journeyed for a short distance, coming out presently at a point where there was a small sheet of water, fed by several brooks. On the edge of the pond—it can scarcely be called a lake—was an Indian village containing perhaps a hundred inhabitants. It was known as Shanorison, and here dwelt an aged chief named Mamuliekala, looked up to by many of the red men because he had once made a trip to Boston and to England. Mamuliekala never ceased to tell of the wonders of the land across the ocean, but only a handful of the red men believed all he said, contending that the English and the rolling of the ship on the ocean had cast a spell over his mind, so that his eyes had deceived him.

Having been brought into Shanorison, Dave was brought before one of the under chiefs, and his captors told their tale. The talking was in a dialect the young pioneer could not understand, and he was asked no questions. Then one of the Indians took him by the arm and led him away.

"What are you going to do with me?" asked the youth.

"Hold white young man a prisoner," was the answer.

"What for?"

"The white young man must tell Pontiac how he came into the cave under the waterfall."

"Did you see any other white people there?"

"Moon Head cannot answer that question," said the Indian.

In the center of the village was a small and rather dirty wigwam, and in this Dave was placed. His hands were kept fastened behind him, and also tied to a short post in the center of the shelter.

"If the young man attempts to escape, he will be killed like a dog," said the Indian, on departing.

"When will Pontiac be here?" called Dave after him, but to this the red man made no reply. He stalked away, letting the flap of the wigwam close after him.

If Dave felt sick in body, he was doubly so in mind. The expedition to the east had come to a sudden and unexpected termination, and what was to be the real end of the adventure there was no telling. Certain it was that Pontiac would be very angry when he learned that the secret he and his followers had guarded so closely was known to the English, and Dave felt that it might go very hard with him in consequence.

"Perhaps they'll burn me at the stake, or do something equally bad," he thought dismally. "I must say, I wish I was out of it. I wonder if I can't manage to escape?"

Edward Stratemeyer

CHAPTER XXIX

PONTIAC'S TRAIL ONCE MORE

The fight between the Indians and the party under Barringford and White Buffalo had been short and sharp. Finding they could not open the passageway to the chamber in which Dave was, as they supposed, entombed alive, the old frontiersman and the Indian chief had returned to the outer world, hoping to find another entrance to the cave. In the midst of the search the enemy had fallen upon them, and the slaughter of the Indians under White Buffalo had occurred.

Pontiac's braves had suffered also, but to what extent Barringford and White Buffalo could not tell. Barringford was wounded in both the thigh and the back, but fortunately neither hurt was serious. White Buffalo received a bullet through the forearm and a cut from a tomahawk, yet with the adroitness of his race he managed to flee with the old frontiersman, and both, after much difficulty, managed to elude their pursuers.

"We must return to Fort Pitt and tell the commander there of what has happened," said Barringford, and White Buffalo agreed. Their horses were gone, so they had to return on foot, the journey taking them two days.

Fort Pitt, it may be mentioned here, was at the time commanded by Captain Simeon Ecuyer, a brave officer, of Swiss birth, who had served the colonies well for years. He listened to Barringford's tale with close attention and keen interest.

"I have suspected something of this sort for a long while," he said. "It was known that many guns and pistols were stolen at the time of General Braddock's defeat, and also during the battles further to the north. I will send out a party at once, and if we can capture the Indians I will see to it that justice is done."

"Bring along picks and spades," said the old frontiersman. "We must save Dave Morris, if the deed is possible."

A company eighteen strong and fully armed left the fort that very noon. Two sharpshooters were in advance, but none of the enemy put in an appearance. Arriving at the waterfall, they found the spot totally deserted. Roaming the forest were two of the horses and these were easily captured, and, later on, one more animal was secured.

"Well, this beats anything I have ever seen!" declared the lieutenant who was in command of the soldiers, after following Barringford into the cave. "It's a perfect treasure house."

"Pray do me the kindness to lose no time in clearing out that passageway," responded Barringford, and under his directions the soldiers set to work with picks and spades and various other entrenching tools to remove the fallen rocks and dirt.

It was a hard task, but inside of three hours the way was cleared and Barringford crawled through, followed by White Buffalo.

"Gone!" murmured the old frontiersman, with a sigh of relief. "I am mighty glad of it."

"White Buffalo glad too," returned the Indian chief simply. "Let us look for his trail."

Plenty of torches were at hand and also a lantern, making the rocky chamber almost as bright as day. With ease the Indian chief traced Dave's footsteps to the split in the rocks, and then hauled himself out through the opening by the tree roots, followed by Barringford.

"This is the way he got out," said the old frontiersman. "But why didn't he return to the waterfall?"

"Fight here," was the red man's answer, pointing to the footprints in the soil. "Two Indians come up behind Dave. Come!"

They left the vicinity, and soon both reached the conclusion that the young pioneer had been carried away a prisoner.

"But where did they take him to?" questioned Barringford.

"We must follow the trail," was all White Buffalo could answer.

A conference was held with the lieutenant, and it was decided that the whole party should follow the trail.

"We can come back to the cave for the goods later," said Lieutenant Peterson. "We certainly must rescue young Morris and make an example of those who have carried him off."

It was no light task to follow the Indian trail through the woods. With all the cuteness of which they were capable, the followers of Pontiac had taken to a shallow stream for over quarter of a mile, and before the trail could be discovered again night came on. They tried to keep up the hunt with torches, but it was of no avail.

"Beaten," muttered Barringford, and his eyes grew moist. "Poor Dave! What will become of him?"

With the coming of morning the lieutenant decided to return to the waterfall. An examination was made, and it was found to be an easy task to make the water flow in another direction, thus leaving the main entrance to the cave a dry one. Without delay the things inside were removed, and loaded on horses. In this manner everything was sooner or later removed to Fort Pitt.

"I shall report to the authorities without delay," said Captain Ecuyer. "More than likely you will be well rewarded for this discovery." But no reward was ever received.

"Never mind the reward," answered Barringford. "I want to find Dave Morris."

"At present I cannot send out another detachment, Barringford. But I will do so in a few days."

"Then I'll take time by the forelock and let his father know what has happened."

"I believe I should do so, were I in your place."

Barringford had had his wounds washed and dressed, and, mounted on a fresh horse, he lost no time in riding back to the trading-post on the Ohio. White Buffalo did not go with him, stating he would renew the hunt for the lost trail.

Edward Stratemeyer

It was Henry who met the old frontiersman at the stockade gate.

"What's wrong?" he questioned quickly. "Where is Dave?"

Before Barringford had time to answer, James Morris showed himself.

"Something has gone wrong!" he cried. "I can see it in your face. What is it?"

"We had a brush with the Indians,—part of Pontiac's party," said the old frontiersman.

"And Dave?"

"We think he was made a prisoner," went on Barringford, and then told his story in detail.

"And you say White Buffalo has gone out again to look for the lost trail?" questioned the trader.

"Yes. He'll find it, too, if it is to be done. I thought you'd like to know, so that you could go out with me and the soldiers."

"Yes! yes!"

"I'd like to go myself, Uncle James," put in Henry.

"One of us ought to remain at the post, Henry. I do not like to leave it in the hands of strangers."

"But they are not all strangers," pleaded Henry. "Some of the men we know very well. We can leave Sanderson in charge. He knows what to do, and so does Jadwin."

"Well, I'll see about it," said Mr. Morris.

As Barringford was hungry, a hasty meal was prepared for him, and then the Morrises had a talk with Sanderson, Jadwin, and some of the others. As a result, Sanderson said he would take charge of the trading-post for a week or longer, if necessary, and Jadwin said he would also remain close at hand, in case he was wanted.

This left Henry free to join Mr. Morris and Barringford in the hunt for Dave, and the young pioneer was not long in preparing himself for the expedition. Fresh horses were obtained, and the party set off early the following morning, when the sun had not yet shown itself over the rolling hills to the eastward.

The day had promised fair, but about noon the sky grew dark very suddenly, and soon after this came a flurry of snow, followed by a heavy wind which tore through the trees of the forest with a mighty roar, hurling more than one trunk to the ground. Broken branches fell in all directions, one hitting Henry on the head and scaring his steed so that the animal could scarcely be controlled.

"I must say I don't like this much!" panted the young pioneer, as he reined in the horse. "What is it, a tornado?"

"We'll have to get behind some rocks for the present," declared Barringford, and this was done. The fierce wind continued for half an hour longer and then subsided. More snow followed, but then came sunshine, as bright and fair as one would wish.

"Only a squall after all," said James Morris. "But it was heavy while it lasted."

When the party arrived at Fort Pitt they found the soldiers

Edward Stratemeyer

ready to go out once more. But nothing had been heard of White Buffalo, which all thought rather strange.

"Perhaps he has failed to recover the trail," said James Morris sorrowfully. "With all his sagacity, White Buffalo cannot do the impossible."

"Do you think it impossible to recover such a trail?" asked Lieutenant Peterson.

"He'll find it—if you give him time enough," put in Barringford confidently. "No Injun better nor White Buffalo on a trail."

"I believe that," said Henry. "He's as smart as they make 'em."

Two hours after this White Buffalo came in. He was plainly tired out, but his face brightened on seeing the whites he knew so well.

"White Buffalo has found the trail," he announced. "It leads to the village of Shanorison, where lives the old chief Mamuliekala, the Great Water Bear. Mamuliekala and Pontiac are like brothers. They have made Dave their prisoner."

"Do you know where Dave is now?"

"White Buffalo has not seen his white brother, but thinks Dave is at the village, or close to it. But we must hurry, for soon Pontiac and his braves will go northward, to the land of the Wyandots and the Ottawas."

"Will they take Dave, or kill him?" asked Henry.

At this the Indian chief shrugged his shoulders.

"Who can answer for the future?" he said briefly.

"Let us be on the way!" cried James Morris impatiently. "An hour lost may mean much to my son!"

"Did the Indians at the village see you?" questioned Captain Ecuyer of the Indian chief.

"No, White Buffalo showed not himself, for it would not have been wise."

While the soldiers were preparing for the new expedition, the Indian chief was given food and drink, after which he said he felt much better. He was provided with a fresh horse to mount, and said he would take a nap in the saddle, a common trick even among red men of to-day. This may appear strange to some of my young readers, but in our army it is well known that men have slept both in the saddle and while on the march!

When the soldiers were assembled, Captain Ecuyer addressed them briefly:

"Men," said he, "you are embarking on rather a dangerous mission. I am sorry I cannot be with you, but it is my duty to remain at the fort, for there may be a general uprising, of which we know nothing. I expect every man to obey Lieutenant Peterson thoroughly, and I want all to do their duty to the uttermost. If you can avoid bloodshed do so, but do not let Pontiac or his followers lead you into any trap. If you are needed at the fort I shall send a messenger after you, and then you must return with all possible speed, for, no matter what else happens, Fort Pitt must not be taken from us."

The men gave a little cheer, and in two minutes the line of march was taken up, some sharpshooters and Barringford leading the way, with James Morris and Henry not far behind. Once again they turned into the mighty forest, heading now directly for the village of Shanorison. Mr. Morris was very anxious to push ahead with all speed, but the soldiers would not go beyond their regular gait.

"Let us go ahead," said he at last, to Henry. "I cannot stand this suspense."

"I'm willing enough," answered his nephew. "Only let us take Sam along."

This was done, and despite the protests of the sharpshooters they were soon out of sight. A little later White Buffalo joined them, having taken the nap already mentioned.

The trail was just as difficult to follow as before, and more than once they had to halt in perplexity, for the thickets seemed impassable.

"You must have had your own troubles in following the trail," said Henry to White Buffalo, in admiration.

"Slow work, but sure," said the Indian chief, with a little smile. "White Buffalo is growing old—he cannot follow like one whose eyes are bright."

At last they reached the cliff. Not wishing to abandon their horses, they made a detour, coming up to the Indian village by what might be termed a back way. In a thicket they tethered their steeds and once on foot each inspected his weapon to see that it was ready for use.

"Don't want any trip-up this time," said Henry, to the flint-lock he carried. "You have played me tricks enough. After this I want you to behave yourself."

It was decided that James Morris and White Buffalo should go slightly in advance—the Indian chief to point out the different parts of the village. Luckily no dogs were near to betray their approach.

To their amazement they found the village practically abandoned, only the women and children and a few very old men being present. The old chief, Mamuliekala, was likewise gone.

"What can this mean?" questioned James Morris.

"It means that the braves have flown, as fly the birds at the coming of winter," answered White Buffalo.

"Let us set a watch and make sure."

Barringford and Henry were called up, and all moved slowly from one outskirt of the village to another. Then they marched forward boldly, arousing several sleeping dogs, who began to bark loudly.

A cry went up from one of the squaws who had a pappoose in her arms, and at this half a dozen squaws and two old men showed themselves.

"Where is Mamuliekala, the Great Water Bear?" asked White Buffalo sternly.

"He has gone on a journey," answered one of the old men, his eyes shifting uneasily as he spoke.

"And where is the white prisoner who was here?"

The old man hesitated and looked for aid from the other aged Indian.

Edward Stratemeyer

"There was no white prisoner here," said the second old Indian.

"Are you so old that you cannot remember," said White Buffalo sternly. "The white prisoner was here. Where has he gone? Answer without delay!"

"Long Knife knows not. He has been sick and asleep. When he awoke Mamuliekala and many of the braves were gone."

This was all the old man would say, and the other aged Indian said he had been away in the woods, digging roots and herbs, for three days. The stories were probably not true, but nothing was to be gained by cross-examining the pair, and White Buffalo did not try it.

"Let us search the village, and question the squaws," said he, and this was done without delay. At first but little could be learned, but at last they made out that Pontiac had been there, and also Foot-in-His-Mouth, and both had gone off during the night with Mamuliekala, taking the braves and some young white person with them. One squaw said that Foot-in-His-Mouth had said the white young man was a runaway soldier and that Pontiac meant to take him to the Fort at Detroit and claim a reward for the service.

"It was a trick—if the story is true," said James Morris.

"True or not, they certainly have taken Dave away," answered Barringford. "And that being so, all we can do is to follow them."

CHAPTER XXX

IN THE CAMP OF THE ENEMY

To Dave, in the dark and foul-smelling wigwam, the time passed slowly. His mind was busy, wondering what the Indians meant to do with him. That they were enraged over the discovery of the underground storehouse was very evident. He heard them talking earnestly among themselves, but what was said, or what conclusion was reached, he could not ascertain.

Late in the evening an Indian girl brought him something to eat and a jug of water. She was rather handsome, with her glossy hair and deep dreamy eyes, and Dave wanted very much to question her. But she could speak no English, and merely shook her head and smiled when he spoke to her.

"I don't think she would try to harm me," he mused. "Wonder if I could get her to aid me?" But this last question remained unanswered, for the young pioneer never saw the Indian maiden again.

Having slipped to the bottom of the post, he fell into a troubled sleep, from which he was rudely awakened by a light kick in the side. An Indian stood there, gazing at him speculatively.

Edward Stratemeyer

"White young man stand up and come along," grunted the red man, and released him from the post.

With stiff arms and shoulders, and knees that did not wish to move, Dave walked from the wigwam. It was early morning, and near a small camp-fire were assembled Foot-in-His-Mouth, Mamuliekala, and several others. They were eating the first meal of the day, and Dave was given a fair share of the food. When he started to talk, he was told to keep silent, and after that saw it would be useless, for the present, to say more.

The meal over, the Indians brought forth a number of horses, and soon the whole party were leaving the village, being followed by a number of braves Dave had not seen before. It was cold and raw, and the wind blew freely and more than once came a flurry of snow.

By the middle of the afternoon the party reached another village called White Bear Spring, tradition telling that a white bear had once had his den close to the spring which fed the brook that was at hand. There was but a small collection of wigwams here, and the place seemed more than half asleep when Dave and his captors came in.

While on horseback the young pioneer's hands had remained free, so that he might guide the steed through the forest and along the river bank. But now, when he dismounted, his hands were again bound behind him.

"White young man try to run away, Indian kill," said Foot-in-His-Mouth, with a frown, and after that Dave was allowed to move around the camp-fire as pleased him. But if he tried to edge toward the boundary of the village he was at once ordered back in a manner that left no room for dispute.

"They don't intend to let me get away," he thought dismally. "And yet, what good will it do them to carry me off?"

It was easy to ask himself this question, but no answer could be reached, and at length he had to give it up. He noticed that some Indians were sent out as guards and he knew that the red men were fearful that somebody had followed them.

The night was passed at White Bear Spring, and the following day the Indians split up into two parties, one moving back to the southward and the other continuing to the north. With the latter contingent went Dave and Foot-in-His-Mouth. The Indian had a long talk with Mamuliekala, and Dave saw a string of wampum passed from the old magician to the other. He also heard Pontiac's name mentioned.

A hard journey on foot now followed. The trail was over rocks and uneven ground, and more than once the young pioneer slipped and fell. The Indians were in no good humor and often pushed and struck him, urging him forward. They did not stop for dinner, and the day's tramp was not concluded until an hour after sunset, when they reached a small valley, wherein flowed a stream on its way to Lake Erie.

The coming of Foot-in-His-Mouth to this place was hailed with delight by the Indians who had erected a village there. Here were a number of huts and log cabins, showing that the red men had gone into winter quarters. Dave was thrust into a hut and told to make himself comfortable on a bundle of robes that were both dirty and full of vermin. He was given a scant supper, and in the morning his breakfast was no more substantial, and even worse cooked.

Several days followed in which nothing out of the ordinary

occurred. Dave was occasionally given the freedom of the camp, at which times two braves were set to watch him. At other times, and during the night, he was forced to keep in the hut, while a red man, young or old, sat on guard at the doorway.

Winter was now coming forward rapidly, and one morning, he awoke to find the ground covered with snow to a depth of several inches. Some additional Indians had come in during the night, and the village was full of life in consequence.

Among the newcomers was Flat Nose, the rascal who had aided Jean Bevoir and Jacques Valette to make the raid on the Morris pack-train. Flat Nose listened with interest to all the other red men had to tell him, and looked at Dave when the young pioneer was eating his dinner. Then Flat Nose left the camp in a hurry, stating that he would be back the next day.

Twelve miles away was a trading-post, which in years gone by had been erected by a Frenchman named Camboyne. The Frenchman had been slain by some Indians, and for three years the post had been deserted, many white hunters and many red men believing it to be haunted. But some Indians who had not heard the story of ghosts came along once and stopped at the post, and after that Indians and whites came and went as pleased them. But everybody was afraid to do any harm to the place, or to take permanent possession, and there the dilapidated building stood until about the time of the Revolution, when a windstorm razed it to the ground.

To the so-called haunted post went Flat Nose, where he joined half a dozen of his followers of the Wanderers.

"What has become of our white brothers, Bevoir and

Valette?" he asked of a fellow warrior, in his native tongue.

"They have gone away, but will be back before the sun is down," was the answer. "Why does Flat Nose ask the question?"

"I bring news of importance. The Wyandots have in their village the son of James Morris, he who has settled upon the Ohio."

"A prisoner, or to trade?"

"A prisoner. Where he was captured they will not tell, but Flat Nose thinks it must have been miles from here."

"Was Pontiac of the Ottawas at the village?" asked the other Indian.

"He was looked for by sunset. That is why I have hurried to see Jean Bevoir and his men. They may wish to question the Wyandots and Pontiac concerning young Morris."

"And what about word to fall upon the whites and slay them?"

"The time is not yet ripe, such was the word given to me by Foot-in-His-Mouth. Many of the Indians are not yet ready for the war."

"Bah! we shall never be ready!" cried the other red man in disgust, and turned away.

For the rest of the day Flat Nose waited impatiently for the coming of Bevoir and Jacques Valette. When at last he saw them approaching he ran to meet them.

As best he could he related what he had seen and heard at

the Indian village. Jacques Valette listened in moody silence, but ere Flat Nose had finished a crafty look came into Jean Bevoir's face.

"Ha, it will be a master stroke!" he cried, in French. "A master stroke—if only I can get this Dave Morris in my power! Flat Nose did well to tell me."

"Perhaps we shall burn our fingers" growled Jacques Valette, who was none the brighter for having drank several glasses of liquor that afternoon.

"No, no, Jacques! Not if we keep our wits about us. I must find out why they have made him their prisoner!"

"And what think you to do then?" asked Valette, exhibiting some interest at last.

"Think? Can you not see? If Pontiac will only turn the youth over to our tender mercies, we shall hold all of the Morrises in our power."

"I see not how."

"Jacques, you are growing stupid. 'Tis as clear as glass. We are becoming hard pressed. Glotte has disappeared and Bergerac has deserted us and gone over to the enemy—"

"He should have his neck wrung for him!" muttered Valette.

"I agree. He has most likely told them everything. The English are in power—"

"But not for long, Jean, not for long!"

"About that I am not so sure. The news from France would seem to point to the fact that our country will give up everything for the sake of peace. Half of the red men are already the friends of the English, and more will follow, if France does nothing to aid Pontiac and his followers."

"Pontiac is strong—he will strike a terrible blow when all his plans are complete."

"I think that myself. But he is not yet ready, and when he is, he may find the English too strong for him. And if Pontiac fails, what will become of us? We shall be hunted down, smoked out, tracked to our final stopping place—and hanged!"

"You are a true comforter, upon my word!"

"I am not one to throw dust into my own eyes, Jacques. Can I not see what is taking place around us? Even many of our old friends shun us, not only our own countrymen, but also the Indians. They see how the wind is blowing."

"With this Dave Morris in your power, what will you do?" questioned Jacques Valette after a pause, during which Jean Bevoir began to walk up and down nervously.

"With him in our power, we shall be safe. Yes, we may even dictate terms to James Morris, the father. He will do anything to save his son—his only child."

"You mean that you will make him promise not to prosecute us?"

"Yes, and more, perhaps."

"What more?"

Jean Bevoir closed one eye suggestively.

"Leave that to me, Jacques. The plan is not yet clear in my mind. But one thing is certain: James Morris will do anything to save his son from harm."

"But what of that Henry Morris, and that old hunter, Barringford?"

"Both will do as James Morris wishes, for one is his nephew and the other a very close friend of the family."

"You may not be able to handle Pontiac."

"That, of course, remains to be seen. It is possible he may be glad enough to get rid of the prisoner. The game is worth the trying," went on Jean Bevoir. "And if Pontiac will not give Morris up, I have another plan," he added suddenly.

"What is that?"

"Time enough to speak of it if Pontiac refuses my request, Jacques. But I must not lose time here. Every hour may count. Will you go to the village with me, or remain with Flat Nose?"

"I will go along," answered Jacques Valette; and soon the wily pair set out on their mission.

CHAPTER XXXI

HELD AS A SPY

Two hours after Flat Nose left the Indian village several Ottawas came in to announce the coming of Pontiac. At once there was a fresh stir and everything possible was done to give the great chief a proper reception. When he appeared the head of the Wyandot tribe went forward to greet him, and both sat down in front of the main log cabin of the village to smoke and to talk.

The conference lasted but a short quarter of an hour, and then Pontiac had himself conducted to the hut in which Dave was a prisoner.

"The white young man is sorry to be a prisoner," he said slowly, and gazing searchingly into the young pioneer's eyes.

"I am sorry," answered Dave simply. "I do not understand it. Are not the English and the red men now at peace with each other?"

"'Tis true, but the white young man has not treated the Indians fairly."

"What have I done that was wrong?"

"The white young man has the eyes of a hawk; he has seen into places that are dark and secret. Such sights are not good for him."

"If you mean the cave under the waterfall, let me ask, why did you have those guns and pistols, and the powder, that belong to the English, stored there?"

"The English owe the poor Indians much—they will not pay. Hence the Indians thought it no more than fair to keep the goods."

Not wishing to anger the great chief too much, Dave did not reply to this.

"The white young man has the eyes of a hawk and the cunning of a fox," continued Pontiac. "He is no trapper, no hunter, no trader, but a spy."

"A spy!" cried Dave, a light breaking in upon him. "So you take me to be a spy?"

"And Pontiac is right. 'Tis useless to deny it. The young man would spy upon the Indians and then go and tell the great English general of what he has seen. He is a snake in the grass, close to the trail of Pontiac and his followers."

"I am not a spy, Chief Pontiac. My father is a trader and I help him at his trading-post on the Ohio, that is all."

Pontiac waved his hand. "The wind can blow a lie away, but the truth is like a rock that the wind cannot stir. Pontiac's followers have watched the white youth, and he knows."

"Chief Pontiac is mistaken, I give him my word upon it," answered Dave. And then he added. "What do you propose to do with me?"

"That remains to be seen. In war times the English and the French put a spy to death. It may be that Pontiac will be more merciful. But first the white young man must tell all he knows."

"Of what?"

"Of the secrets of the Indians, and of their plans."

"I know next to nothing. I understand but little of the language."

"And what of the plans of the English?"

"You mean of our soldiers?"

"Of the soldiers and of those who command them."

"I know absolutely nothing about our soldiers. I was in the army at the fall of Montreal, but after that I was mustered out and I went back to my regular work on the farm, and to hunting and fishing."

"You were at the fort at Niagara."

"Yes, I was there, too, before I went down the St. Lawrence."

"And still you say you are not a spy? The fox is sly, but not so sly as Pontiac supposed." "I tell you, once for all, I am not a spy, Chief Pontiac."

The celebrated Indian chief drew himself up and gave Dave a long, earnest look. He evidently saw that the young pioneer meant what he said. He was about to speak, to offer Dave a chance to return home. But then he remembered what had happened at the underground storehouse,

Edward Stratemeyer

and hesitated.

"Pontiac will see the white young man again," he said briefly, and left as abruptly as he had come.

The conversation made Dave more uneasy in mind than before. He had not thought that the red men would consider him a spy. If they continued to do that, it might go extra hard with him in the near future. Pontiac had said that the French and the English put a spy to death, but he had not added that the Indians frequently took a spy and tortured him most cruelly, yet such was a fact. Only two years before a spy had been caught by the Indians near the Great Lakes, and it was a matter of record that the red men had placed him upon the ground flat on his back and built a fire upon his breast, leaving him to burn slowly to death! The thought of this sent a cold shiver down Dave's backbone.

"I hope they don't torture me!" he muttered. "Oh, anything but that!" There was no consolation in the thought that Pontiac had said he might be more merciful than the French or English. He knew how cruel all red men could be when their evil passions were aroused.

When Pontiac came away from his interview with Dave, he was beyond a doubt in a quandary. His plans against the English were many, and evidently he was much worried, thinking Dave knew much more than was the fact. It had galled him to let the summer pass without striking the cherished blow, but he had great hopes for the summer to come; and history has already recorded what he did shortly after the time of which I am now writing.

Pontiac was in deep thought when a young brave came to him and said two French hunters wished to speak to him. Thinking they might have news of value, he consented to the interview, and was soon in conversation with Jean Bevoir and Jacques Valette.

Of Bevoir Pontiac had heard several times. He knew the French trader to be a two-faced rascal, and probably he despised him accordingly, for, judged solely by Indian standards, Pontiac was an upright and honest man. His duplicity was only that of the red man when on the war-path. In his personal dealing he would not have cheated a fellow Indian or a white man out of a farthing.

Jean Bevoir was not long in coming to the point.

He said he had heard that Dave Morris had been made a prisoner by the Indians. If Pontiac wanted to get rid of the young fellow he, Bevoir, would take him off his hands and be glad to do it.

"But what will my French friend do with this Morris?" asked Pontiac.

"Leave that to me," answered Bevoir. "I'll take good care that he does not bother you again."

By skillful questioning Pontiac managed to learn a great deal of what was in Bevoir's mind, and he saw at once that the Frenchman was indeed an enemy to the young pioneer. Then Valette began to talk, saying Morris should never cross the path of the Indians again, once he and Bevoir got their hands upon him.

"Pontiac wishes him to live," said the chief shrewdly.

"He shall not die," said Bevoir. "But we shall take care that he comes not to this neighborhood again."

Pontiac said he would think it over. He felt certain that

Bevoir and Valette were up to some foul deed, and was half inclined to send them from the village.

"While Pontiac thinks it over can I speak to the prisoner?" asked Jean Bevoir.

After some hesitation Pontiac allowed him to see Dave, and soon the two were face to face in the hut. Pontiac wished to set a spy to listen to what was said, but another matter claimed his attention.

"Jean Bevoir!" cried Dave. "What brings you to this place?"

"Not so loud!" answered Jean Bevoir in a whisper. "Morris, I am your friend, believe me."

"My friend?" ejaculated the young pioneer.

"*Oui!* Listen! The Indians wish to kill you. I wish to save you. If I do that, will you—you—"

"What?"

"Will you promise to go to your father and tell him I have saved you?"

"Why do you want that?"

"We are now enemies. I wish to be friends. He will be a friend to one who saves his son's life."

"Perhaps, Bevoir." Dave's head was in a whirl. "But this,— of you! I can scarcely believe it! And then that attack on the pack-train!"

"Was Hector Bergerac's work! I can prove it! Come, shall I save you or not?"

"Yes, save me if you can," muttered Dave.

"And you will tell your father of it?"

"Yes."

"Then listen. Here is a sharp hunting knife. See, I will stick it between the logs, so that you may cut your cords with it. To-night when you hear the owl hoot, free yourself and steal from the hut, if you can. Follow the hoot of the owl and I will be there with swift horses."

"And then?" asked the young pioneer.

"We will away, straight for your father's trading-post." Jean Bevoir paused a moment. "It may be I can persuade Pontiac to give you up. If I can, so much the better. But if not, remember what I have told you. If Pontiac asks you if you will go with me, say yes."

"I may be shot down if I try to escape in the dark."

"You must take the risk." Bevoir came closer. "They mean to burn you at the stake, to-morrow at noon,—I heard the talk an hour ago," he went on, in a low tone.

"I'll escape if I can," said Dave; and a moment later Jean Bevoir left him.

The young pioneer's thoughts were in a tumult. He did not believe in Bevoir, yet what the man said might possibly be true. He did not wish to be tortured by the Indians.

"I'd rather run my chances with Bevoir," he told himself. "I'll have the knife, and perhaps I can pick up a gun or a pistol. He may be sick of hiding himself, and he knows father will treat him kindly if he really does save me."

Dave had not seen Jacques Valette, and he fancied he was to meet Jean Bevoir alone. It would be dark, and perhaps he could slip away from the Frenchman as well as from the Indians. Anyway, the plan appeared to be worth trying.

Pontiac had expected to remain at the village over night, but at sunset a messenger came for him to meet some other chiefs several miles away. He departed hastily, leaving Dave in charge of Foot-in-His-Mouth and the Wyandots.

When Jean Bevoir saw Pontiac depart he was glad that he had spoken to Dave about escaping. He felt certain the young pioneer would fall into the trap. He and Valette left the camp together, and at once summoned Flat Nose and the other Indians who were in their employ.

"Once let me get Dave Morris in my power and all will be well," said Jean Bevoir exultantly. He was in such high spirits he could scarcely wait for night to come,

"Where will you take him?" questioned Valette.

"To the westward, where I know we shall be safe."

"And after that?"

"I shall negotiate with James Morris," chuckled Bevoir. "Oh, but I shall bring him to terms!"

At last it grew dark. There was a promise of a storm in the air and soon the snow began to come down. This did not suit Bevoir, for it would make tracking easy, but as this could not be avoided, he determined to make the best of it. Should it continue to snow, the tracks made during the night would soon be obliterated.

CHAPTER XXXII

A FIGHT AND A VICTORY—CONCLUSION

The news that Dave was not at the Indian village of Shanorison was dismaying to Mr. Morris, Barringford, and Henry, for they had expected beyond a doubt to find the captive there.

"All we can do is to continue on the trail," said James Morris promptly. "I shall not turn back until he is found."

"Nor I," added Henry promptly.

"We're bound to catch 'em some time," came from the old frontiersman. "Don't you think so, White Buffalo?"

"White Buffalo is sure he can overtake those who are fleeing," answered the chief. "But it may take many days."

Lieutenant Peterson was consulted and he said he would follow the trail for one day longer.

"After that, I will have to turn back," he continued. "I have strict orders to go but so far from Fort Pitt, and no further. You see we may be needed there, if the redskins contemplate an attack." "That is true," said James Morris. "I should like to have you with us, but orders are orders.

Edward Stratemeyer

"I will detail two of my best shots to go with your party, Mr. Morris. They are men who are used to fighting the redskins in their own way, and will be of great assistance."

The day passed slowly, but when the sun went down no Indians had been seen. The little party went into camp under the shelter of some trees, and in the early morning Lieutenant Peterson set out on the return to Fort Pitt, leaving behind the two sharpshooters as he had promised.

"And now to go it alone!" cried Henry. "Perhaps we'll do better than with so many soldiers behind us."

"We can certainly continue the hunt with less chance of being observed," answered his uncle.

Henry was very impatient to overtake those who had Dave in charge, but the trail was an uncertain one, and once they made a false move which took them some miles out of their true course. This false turn made White Buffalo very angry, and he berated himself roundly for the mistake.

"White Buffalo is getting old," he declared. "He is like a squaw on the trail. He had better go and live with the old women of his tribe."

"Never mind, White Buffalo, we are all liable to make mistakes," said the trader kindly.

At last the Indian chief announced that they had reached fresh tracks, and that they were close to another village. Soon after that Barringford came in and announced that he had seen the trail of some white men, evidently hunters and trappers.

"We must be careful now," said the old frontiersman, "If we ain't, we may run into a reg'lar trap."

The party came to a halt, and soon after that it began to snow, and by the time it was dark the snow covered the ground to the depth of an inch and more.

"That ends trailing," said Barringford. "Hang the luck anyway!"

As the snow continued to come down, they made themselves comfortable under some immense spruce trees whose branches almost touched the ground. Here supper was had, and then Henry and Barringford, accompanied by White Buffalo; moved up to the top of a small hill which was close at hand, hoping to discover something from that point of vantage.

"I see a camp-fire!" cried Henry, who was the first to gain the high ground.

"Yes, an' it ain't more 'n quarter o' mile from here, nuther," came from Barringford. "Tell ye what, boys, I think we've come about to the end o' the trail; eh! White Buffalo?"

"White Buffalo thinks his brother Sam is right," was the slow answer. "'Tis the camp-fire of the Wyandots, and no other camp-fire is near," he added, sweeping the entire distance with his sharp eyes.

"Shall we go forward at once?" questioned the young pioneer eagerly.

"We'll see what your uncle says," returned Barringford.

It did not take them long to consult with James Morris, and as a result, the whole party moved onward once more, with the Morrises, Barringford, and White Buffalo in advance.

This movement occurred on the very night that Dave meant to try for liberty. The knife in the logs was still there, and all unknown to the Indians who were holding him a prisoner, he backed up to it and cut the thongs that bound his hands behind him.

Outside of the hut it was snowing furiously, and the Indian guard did not attempt to pace up and down as usual, but sat under a shelter of bark, smoking and dozing. The Indians did not think that their prisoner would attempt to escape, for on all sides of the village lay the immense forest, inhabited by many savage animals and now fast filling with snow. Unarmed, and unguided, a single person in that region would soon become lost, and most likely perish from hunger.

At last Dave thought it time to make a move. He had not yet heard the signal agreed upon between himself and Jean Bevoir, but he did not wish to wait for this, being even more anxious to escape from the Frenchman than from the red men.

With the hunting knife in his hand, he moved cautiously to the rear of the hut. Here was a small opening which he had discovered the day before. Through it he wormed his way, coming out through the dead leaves and the snow on the outside. A dozen steps away was a fringe of brushwood, and hither he moved, with the silence of a ghost.

As he gained the bushes the hoot of an owl, or rather the imitation thereof, came to his ears. It was the signal, and he knew that Jean Bevoir must be close at hand.

Instead of going directly toward the signal, Dave attempted to go around it. His object in doing this was to get behind Bevoir, obtain one of the horses the Frenchman had mentioned, and be off before Jean Bevoir could stop him.

He knew he would run the risk of being shot should the Frenchman still be treacherous, but hoped that the darkness of the night would favor him.

Again came the hoot of the owl, in the same place as before. Dave was moving around to the southward, trying to pierce the darkness. Between the thick branches of the trees and the snow he could see next to nothing, and almost before he knew it he had stepped into a hollow and gone down a distance of several feet. His knee struck a rock, hurting him severely and causing him to give a gasp of pain.

As Dave was rising a form appeared before him, and an instant later he was confronted by Flat Nose. The Indian came forward before the young pioneer could think of withdrawing.

"White young man here!" cried Flat Nose softly. And he followed this with the call of a night-bird, thrice repeated.

"I want nothing of you!" exclaimed Dave, and started to retreat, when Flat Nose caught him by the arm. But Dave struck out with the hunting knife, and the Indian fell back with a wound in his shoulder. Before he could recover, the young pioneer was running off as swiftly as his hurt knee would permit.

In a moment more Dave heard, not only Flat Nose, but also several others in pursuit. A call reached him in the voice of Jean Bevoir, but to this he paid no attention. He knew that his only safety lay in escape.

But while he was running from Flat Nose and Jean Bevoir he was making directly towards Jacques Valette, and in less than a minute the two came face to face. Valette had his gun handy and the moment the young pioneer appeared he raised the weapon.

Edward Stratemeyer

"Stop!" he roared. "Stop, or I shoot!"

"Do not let him escape!" cried Jean Bevoir, in French.

"I have him safe enough," came from Valette.

Covered by a gun in the hands of such a villain as Jacques Valette, Dave did not know what to do. The fellow looked ready to shoot, and even anxious to pull the trigger.

While he was meditating, Jean Bevoir, Flat Nose, and several Indians of the Wanderers' tribe came up. The young pioneer was immediately surrounded, and Flat Nose caught him around the breast from the rear, pinning his arms to his side. The hunting knife was taken from him, and he realized at once that further resistance would be useless.

"Ha! so you think to escape, not so?" sneered Jean Bevoir. "I was afraid it would be so. But now you are my prisonair, ha! ha!"

"What are you going to do with me?" asked Dave, as calmly as he could, but with a sinking heart.

"You will learn that later, Dave Morris."

"You said you would take me back to my father's trading-post."

"Did you believe zat? Ha! ha! you are a leetle fool! I shall take you to the west, far away, oui! Then your father shall come to terms, not so? He will do anything to geet back his only son."

Like a flash the full realization of Jean Bevoir's plot forced itself upon the young pioneer. He was truly in the hands of the enemy, and it was safe to say that Bevoir would not treat him any better than had Pontiac, if as well.

"Supposing I won't go with you?" he said.

"You shall go with us," replied Jean Bevoir. "You are my prisonair and must do as I say. Jacques, bring up the horses."

Valette turned away to do as bidden. As he did so there came a shout from a distance, followed by a peculiar Indian-cry, telling all in the village that the white captive had escaped.

"We must be quick!" said Bevoir, in French. "There is not a moment to spare."

Jacques Valette brought up the horses with all possible speed. There was one for Dave, and he was hoisted in the saddle, with his hands bound behind him. Then the whole party turned directly westward, toward a trail well known to Flat Nose and his followers.

It was now snowing furiously, and the trail left by the party was quickly covered. In the village the alarm continued, and several of the Wyandots and the red men left behind by Pontiac began a diligent search for the missing prisoner. In the party was Foot-in-His-Mouth, and before long he found the right trail and came in sight of Jacques Valette, who was in the rear.

He had hardly raised his cry of discovery when Valette turned in the saddle, took aim through the falling snow, and fired. His bullet went true, and Foot-in-His-Mouth pitched headlong and lay still forever.

"They are coming!" cried Valette, as he went forward once more. "We shall have to fight for it!"

"No! no! we must escape through the snow!" ejaculated Jean Bevoir. He had not dreamed that the situation would take such a serious turn. "Come! come!"

On they went, faster than ever. The branches of the trees struck Dave in the breast and in the face, and once he was almost thrown from the saddle. They were passing down into an open space, where the snow was blowing furiously. Jean Bevoir hailed the falling flakes with satisfaction. They would surely cover the trail which so badly needed obliteration.

Beyond the open space was another patch of timber. But here the trees were further apart, so progress was easier. On and on they went, with the Wyandots and Ottawas still in pursuit. The horses were almost out of breath, yet were urged to do their utmost by the Frenchmen and the Wanderers, who knew that if the pursuers came up to them a fierce pitched battle would surely result, with perhaps a number killed and wounded on each side.

Dave was tugging at the cords which tied his hands, and now to his satisfaction they came loose, leaving him free. He wondered what he had best do. Should he risk a rush to the right or the left? That would place one set of enemies in front of him and one behind. But all might pass on, leaving him to shift for himself.

While he was deliberating a shout rang out ahead, followed by a rifle shot. Then, as if in a dream, he heard a yell in Sam Barringford's voice:

"Stop, Jean Bevoir, you everlastin' rascal! Stop!"

"Sam! Sam!" he screamed, and rode forward. "Sam, is it really you!"

"Dave!" came in the voice of Henry. "Dave! What can this mean? What are you doing here?"

The cry came from the left, and Dave turned his horse in that direction. More shots rang out, and he saw an Indian go down. Then Jacques Valette turned toward the young pioneer.

"You shall not get away!" cried the rascally French hunter, and raised his gun. But before he could use the weapon James Morris fired upon him, and Valette pitched into the snow, shot through the thigh. Then Dave went on, and in a moment more found himself among his friends and relatives.

There was no time to answer questions. The Wyandots and Ottawas were coming up swiftly, and once more the Wanderers and Jean Bevoir attempted to outdistance them. Jacques Valette also attempted to remount his horse, but ere he could do so a Wyandot reached him and struck him down again. The blow crushed the Frenchman's skull, and he died before sunrise.

"We must get out of this," said Dave, when he could speak. "The Indians are after us! If we stay here we may be caught between two fires."

"Come with me!" came from White Buffalo. "White Buffalo knows a good hiding place."

James Morris' party turned back, and with Dave by his father's side, all rode through the forest to the southward. Here they reached a small brook, backed up by rugged rocks and a thick patch of timber. In the timber they halted, and in a short while the snow, now whirling in every direction, hid their trail completely from view.

Edward Stratemeyer

Listening intently they heard many shots at a distance and knew that a fierce fight was on, between those from the village and the party under Jean Bevoir. The fighting kept on for a good half-hour, then gradually died away to the northward.

Safe in the shelter near the brook, Dave told his story, to which his father, Henry, and the others listened with great interest.

"You can be thankful that we came up as we did" said James Morris.

"I am thankful," said the young pioneer. "I never want to see Jean Bevoir and his rascally companions again."

"Perhaps Jean Bevoir is dead," put in Henry. "That shooting must have meant something."

"I brought down Jacques Valette," continued Mr. Morris. "But I don't believe I killed him."

"I hit Bevoir in the arm," came from Barringford. "He'll remember it a while, I'll warrant."

"It was all Pontiac's fault," came from Dave. "I think the authorities ought to bring him to book for it."

"Perhaps they will," answered James Morris seriously.

Let me add a few words more and then bring to a close this story of pioneer life, and of adventures while "On the Trail of Pontiac."

The snowstorm that started that evening proved a heavy one, and it was not until nearly a week later that the Morris party managed to get back to Fort Pitt. Here the commandant listened to what they had to relate with close attention and said he would report to the proper authorities at the first opportunity. But means of communication were now almost entirely cut off; and in the end little or nothing was done to make Pontiac and his followers explain their actions, matters of greater importance coming up in the meantime.

When they felt able to do so, Dave and Barringford continued on the trip to Will's Creek, taking White Buffalo and some of his followers with them. The others of the party returned to the trading-post, anxious to learn if matters there were quiet. They found no cause for alarm, but a few days later two trappers came in with news that nearly all of the Bevoir party had been killed, Bevoir himself escaping after being wounded both in the arm and the side.

"The Wyandots and the Ottawas are very angry at the Wanderers," said the hunter who furnished the news. "They say the Wanderers must hereafter keep to the hunting grounds in the far west. The Wyandots say there was some mistake made about Dave, and they are going to bring in, next spring, the goods they got away from Bevoir, and which were stolen from the pack-train."

"I trust they keep their word," answered James Morris. "But I reckon that fifty pounds is gone for good."

"I think they will keep their word," said Sanderson, who knew many of the Wyandots well. "They want to be at peace and they'd be all right if only the Ottawas would leave them alone."

"Pontiac will never rest until he has united the Indians in a regular war against the English," said James Morris, and how true his words were will be shown in another volume of this series, to be entitled, "The Fort in the Wilderness; or,

Edward Stratemeyer

The Soldier Boys of the Indian Trails." In this volume we shall meet all of our old friends again, and learn what more was done toward establishing the trading-post on the Ohio, and of how Jean Bevoir again crossed the path of the Morrises and made himself more odious than ever.

The home-coming of Dave was made a joyous time at the Morris cabin. His Aunt Lucy came out to greet him warmly, followed by Rodney and little Nell. The twins stood in the doorway, gazing shyly at him and Sam Barringford.

"I am so glad you are safe!" said Mrs. Morris, as she kissed her nephew.

"And I'm glad myself," answered Dave, but she did not fully understand all he meant until he had told his story.

"Reckon as how this is my family," came from Sam Barringford, as he took one of the twins in each arm. "No news of 'em, is thar?" he asked.

"No news, Sam," said Rodney. "Reckon they are yours right enough." But Rodney was mistaken, as later events proved.

"Well, I'll try to give 'em a father's care," went on the old frontiersman. And he gave each twin a half-dozen hugs and kisses, at which both crowed loudly. They were the pets of the household and all loved them dearly.

"You can't imagine how good it feels to be at home once more," said Dave, later on. "The trading-post is all well enough, but it can't touch a place like this."

"If all goes well, I am going out to the trading-post next year," came from Rodney. "I am now as strong as any of you."

"Do not talk of spring yet," said Mrs. Morris. "We have still a long, hard winter to face."

What she said was true, and winter started in earnest the very next day, snowing for the best part of a week, and then turning off bitterly cold. Yet firewood was to be had in plenty and the cabin was kept warm and comfortable for all.

"We've had some great times this past season," said Barringford, as he warmed himself by the cheerful kitchen blaze. "Great times, eh, White Buffalo?"

The Indian chief, who had come in to smoke a friendly pipe, nodded. "My brother Sam is right," he said. "But all has gone well, so let us be thankful."

"Yes, let us be thankful," came from Dave.

And they were thankful; and here let us leave them, wishing them the best of luck for the future.

Edward Stratemeyer

Choose from Thousands of 1stWorldLibrary Classics By

A. M. Barnard
Ada Leverson
Adolphus William Ward
Aesop
Agatha Christie
Alexander Aaronsohn
Alexander Kielland
Alexandre Dumas
Alfred Gatty
Alfred Ollivant
Alice Duer Miller
Alice Turner Curtis
Alice Dunbar
Allen Chapman
Alleyne Ireland
Ambrose Bierce
Amelia E. Barr
Amory H. Bradford
Andrew Lang
Andrew McFarland Davis
Andy Adams
Angela Brazil
Anna Alice Chapin
Anna Sewell
Annie Besant
Annie Hamilton Donnell
Annie Payson Call
Annie Roe Carr
Annonaymous
Anton Chekhov
Archibald Lee Fletcher
Arnold Bennett
Arthur C. Benson
Arthur Conan Doyle
Arthur M. Winfield
Arthur Ransome
Arthur Schnitzler
Arthur Train
Atticus
B.H. Baden-Powell
B. M. Bower
B. C. Chatterjee
Baroness Emmuska Orczy
Baroness Orczy
Basil King
Bayard Taylor
Ben Macomber
Bertha Muzzy Bower
Bjornstjerne Bjornson

Booth Tarkington
Boyd Cable
Bram Stoker
C. Collodi
C. E. Orr
C. M. Ingleby
Carolyn Wells
Catherine Parr Traill
Charles A. Eastman
Charles Amory Beach
Charles Dickens
Charles Dudley Warner
Charles Farrar Browne
Charles Ives
Charles Kingsley
Charles Klein
Charles Hanson Towne
Charles Lathrop Pack
Charles Romyn Dake
Charles Whibley
Charles Willing Beale
Charlotte M. Braeme
Charlotte M. Yonge
Charlotte Perkins Stetson
Clair W. Hayes
Clarence Day Jr.
Clarence E. Mulford
Clemence Housman
Confucius
Coningsby Dawson
Cornelis DeWitt Wilcox
Cyril Burleigh
D. H. Lawrence
Daniel Defoe
David Garnett
Dinah Craik
Don Carlos Janes
Donald Keyhoe
Dorothy Kilner
Dougan Clark
Douglas Fairbanks
E. Nesbit
E. P. Roe
E. Phillips Oppenheim
E. S. Brooks
Earl Barnes
Edgar Rice Burroughs
Edith Van Dyne
Edith Wharton

Edward Everett Hale
Edward J. O'Biren
Edward S. Ellis
Edwin L. Arnold
Eleanor Atkins
Eleanor Hallowell Abbott
Eliot Gregory
Elizabeth Gaskell
Elizabeth McCracken
Elizabeth Von Arnim
Ellem Key
Emerson Hough
Emilie F. Carlen
Emily Bronte
Emily Dickinson
Enid Bagnold
Enilor Macartney Lane
Erasmus W. Jones
Ernie Howard Pie
Ethel May Dell
Ethel Turner
Ethel Watts Mumford
Eugene Sue
Eugenie Foa
Eugene Wood
Eustace Hale Ball
Evelyn Everett-green
Everard Cotes
F. H. Cheley
F. J. Cross
F. Marion Crawford
Fannie E. Newberry
Federick Austin Ogg
Ferdinand Ossendowski
Fergus Hume
Florence A. Kilpatrick
Fremont B. Deering
Francis Bacon
Francis Darwin
Frances Hodgson Burnett
Frances Parkinson Keyes
Frank Gee Patchin
Frank Harris
Frank Jewett Mather
Frank L. Packard
Frank V. Webster
Frederic Stewart Isham
Frederick Trevor Hill
Frederick Winslow Taylor

Friedrich Kerst
Friedrich Nietzsche
Fyodor Dostoyevsky
G.A. Henty
G.K. Chesterton
Gabrielle E. Jackson
Garrett P. Serviss
Gaston Leroux
George A. Warren
George Ade
Geroge Bernard Shaw
George Cary Eggleston
George Durston
George Ebers
George Eliot
George Gissing
George MacDonald
George Meredith
George Orwell
George Sylvester Viereck
George Tucker
George W. Cable
George Wharton James
Gertrude Atherton
Gordon Casserly
Grace E. King
Grace Gallatin
Grace Greenwood
Grant Allen
Guillermo A. Sherwell
Gulielma Zollinger
Gustav Flaubert
H. A. Cody
H. B. Irving
H.C. Bailey
H. G. Wells
H. H. Munro
H. Irving Hancock
H. R. Naylor
H. Rider Haggard
H. W. C. Davis
Haldeman Julius
Hall Caine
Hamilton Wright Mabie
Hans Christian Andersen
Harold Avery
Harold McGrath
Harriet Beecher Stowe
Harry Castlemon
Harry Coghill
Harry Houidini

Hayden Carruth
Helent Hunt Jackson
Helen Nicolay
Hendrik Conscience
Hendy David Thoreau
Henri Barbusse
Henrik Ibsen
Henry Adams
Henry Ford
Henry Frost
Henry James
Henry Jones Ford
Henry Seton Merriman
Henry W Longfellow
Herbert A. Giles
Herbert Carter
Herbert N. Casson
Herman Hesse
Hildegard G. Frey
Homer
Honore De Balzac
Horace B. Day
Horace Walpole
Horatio Alger Jr.
Howard Pyle
Howard R. Garis
Hugh Lofting
Hugh Walpole
Humphry Ward
Ian Maclaren
Inez Haynes Gillmore
Irving Bacheller
Isabel Cecilia Williams
Isabel Hornibrook
Israel Abrahams
Ivan Turgenev
J.G.Austin
J. Henri Fabre
J. M. Barrie
J. M. Walsh
J. Macdonald Oxley
J. R. Miller
J. S. Fletcher
J. S. Knowles
J. Storer Clouston
J. W. Duffield
Jack London
Jacob Abbott
James Allen
James Andrews
James Baldwin

James Branch Cabell
James DeMille
James Joyce
James Lane Allen
James Lane Allen
James Oliver Curwood
James Oppenheim
James Otis
James R. Driscoll
Jane Abbott
Jane Austen
Jane L. Stewart
Janet Aldridge
Jens Peter Jacobsen
Jerome K. Jerome
Jessie Graham Flower
John Buchan
John Burroughs
John Cournos
John F. Kennedy
John Gay
John Glasworthy
John Habberton
John Joy Bell
John Kendrick Bangs
John Milton
John Philip Sousa
John Taintor Foote
Jonas Lauritz Idemil Lie
Jonathan Swift
Joseph A. Altsheler
Joseph Carey
Joseph Conrad
Joseph E. Badger Jr
Joseph Hergesheimer
Joseph Jacobs
Jules Vernes
Julian Hawthrone
Julie A Lippmann
Justin Huntly McCarthy
Kakuzo Okakura
Karle Wilson Baker
Kate Chopin
Kenneth Grahame
Kenneth McGaffey
Kate Langley Bosher
Kate Langley Bosher
Katherine Cecil Thurston
Katherine Stokes
L. A. Abbot
L. T. Meade

L. Frank Baum
Latta Griswold
Laura Dent Crane
Laura Lee Hope
Laurence Housman
Lawrence Beasley
Leo Tolstoy
Leonid Andreyev
Lewis Carroll
Lewis Sperry Chafer
Lilian Bell
Lloyd Osbourne
Louis Hughes
Louis Joseph Vance
Louis Tracy
Louisa May Alcott
Lucy Fitch Perkins
Lucy Maud Montgomery
Luther Benson
Lydia Miller Middleton
Lyndon Orr
M. Corvus
M. H. Adams
Margaret E. Sangster
Margret Howth
Margaret Vandercook
Margaret W. Hungerford
Margret Penrose
Maria Edgeworth
Maria Thompson Daviess
Mariano Azuela
Marion Polk Angellotti
Mark Overton
Mark Twain
Mary Austin
Mary Catherine Crowley
Mary Cole
Mary Hastings Bradley
Mary Roberts Rinehart
Mary Rowlandson
M. Wollstonecraft Shelley
Maud Lindsay
Max Beerbohm
Myra Kelly
Nathaniel Hawthrone
Nicolo Machiavelli
O. F. Walton
Oscar Wilde

Owen Johnson
P.G. Wodehouse
Paul and Mabel Thorne
Paul G. Tomlinson
Paul Severing
Percy Brebner
Percy Keese Fitzhugh
Peter B. Kyne
Plato
Quincy Allen
R. Derby Holmes
R. L. Stevenson
R. S. Ball
Rabindranath Tagore
Rahul Alvares
Ralph Bonehill
Ralph Henry Barbour
Ralph Victor
Ralph Waldo Emmerson
Rene Descartes
Ray Cummings
Rex Beach
Rex E. Beach
Richard Harding Davis
Richard Jefferies
Richard Le Gallienne
Robert Barr
Robert Frost
Robert Gordon Anderson
Robert L. Drake
Robert Lansing
Robert Lynd
Robert Michael Ballantyne
Robert W. Chambers
Rosa Nouchette Carey
Rudyard Kipling
Saint Augustine
Samuel B. Allison
Samuel Hopkins Adams
Sarah Bernhardt
Sarah C. Hallowell
Selma Lagerlof
Sherwood Anderson
Sigmund Freud
Standish O'Grady
Stanley Weyman
Stella Benson
Stella M. Francis

Stephen Crane
Stewart Edward White
Stijn Streuvels
Swami Abhedananda
Swami Parmananda
T. S. Ackland
T. S. Arthur
The Princess Der Ling
Thomas A. Janvier
Thomas A Kempis
Thomas Anderton
Thomas Bailey Aldrich
Thomas Bulfinch
Thomas De Quincey
Thomas Dixon
Thomas H. Huxley
Thomas Hardy
Thomas More
Thornton W. Burgess
U. S. Grant
Upton Sinclair
Valentine Williams
Various Authors
Vaughan Kester
Victor Appleton
Victor G. Durham
Victoria Cross
Virginia Woolf
Wadsworth Camp
Walter Camp
Walter Scott
Washington Irving
Wilbur Lawton
Wilkie Collins
Willa Cather
Willard F. Baker
William Dean Howells
William le Queux
W. Makepeace Thackeray
William W. Walter
William Shakespeare
Winston Churchill
Yei Theodora Ozaki
Yogi Ramacharaka
Young E. Allison
Zane Grey